Books should be returned or renewed by the 2 MAY 2022
last date stamped above

FUTURE PROMISE

The huge problem of the sale of the garage, their home and livelihood, worried Morag Kinloch. Her father felt his only two options — be a taxi driver for a former apprentice or managing his estranged sister's business — demeaned him. Then the rumour about her young sister's new male lodger added to Morag's anxiety. So Gordon McEwan's reflections on their future had to wait.

BARBARA COWAN

FUTURE PROMISE

Complete and Unabridged

LINFORD
Leicester

First published in Great Britain in 1995

First Linford Edition
published 2005

British Library CIP Data

Cowan, Barbara
    Future promise.—Large print ed.—
    Linford romance library
    1. Love stories
    2. Large type books
    I. Title
    823.9'2 [F]

    ISBN 1–84617–105–9

Published by
F. A. Thorpe (Publishing)
Anstey, Leicestershire

Set by Words & Graphics Ltd.
Anstey, Leicestershire
Printed and bound in Great Britain by
T. J. International Ltd., Padstow, Cornwall

This book is printed on acid-free paper

There's Nothing Else We Can Do

Morag Kinloch watched as the old car drove slowly past the petrol pumps, out of the garage, and on to the road.

The elderly driver scowled at her, and Morag shook her head, half amused, half saddened. As a long-time customer of the garage he seemed to think the family business was closing simply to inconvenience him.

Had he any idea, she mused, of the sorrow and anxiety her family felt at leaving both their home and their livelihood?

For a moment she wondered whether she would miss all the customers like him, now that her family was being forced to close the business?

Yes, she probably would — but not nearly as much as she'd miss the place itself.

1

She'd grown up here, and she knew by heart every inch of the hazy hills in the distance, the sloping fields, the row of trees up on the ridge which hid the town.

It looked at its most appealing just now, as the sun's first golden rays of the day pushed through the mist.

No doubt its beauty was what appealed to the developers, too — why else would they have bought the site, and all it contained, so quickly?

But I won't miss these, Morag thought wryly, looking at her hands covered in oily grease. It would be nice to have a job which didn't involve scrubbing off ingrained dirt every night.

Morag smiled as she pulled open the door of the garage washroom. Her family would be surprised if they knew she felt that way, for they believed she enjoyed working in the garage.

Perhaps it was her own fault, though. When her parents had asked her to leave school and come to work here, instead of going to university, she'd agreed without complaining — because she'd thought it was the only way to save the business.

Yet it seemed now that her sacrifice had been in vain . . .

As Morag washed her hands, she could hear Peggy, the assistant in the garage shop, moving about next door.

'It's your sister Morag I'm sorry for,' Peggy was saying to Morag's young brother, Tom. 'She's given up everything for your dad's business. It's a shame, too — she never seems to have any time to herself. You only need to look at the way she dresses to see that.'

Morag looked at herself critically in the mirror. Could people really tell anything about her from her appearance?

Maybe she was slightly overweight, she considered. And she hadn't had her hair cut for months . . .

'She should have stayed on at school and gone to university, instead of giving it all up to work here as a dogsbody.' Peggy was getting into her stride now.

'Goodness knows she's clever enough.'

Morag felt a pang of disappointment at that. If only Peggy knew how much she'd wanted to stay on at school.

But eight years ago, it had seemed a matter of survival . . .

The garage had just lost its biggest customer with the closure of the local engineering works. The only way to keep the business going was to pay off all the staff and for the family to run the garage on their own.

Morag dried her hands, then breezed out into the shop, enjoying Peggy's abashed look as the older woman realised she'd been overheard.

She was surprised to see the tall, thin figure of Gordon McEwan standing with Peggy and Tom.

'Hello, Morag,' Gordon said. 'I just called in to see if you'd had any more news.'

'It's been confirmed,' she told him flatly. 'The garage closes at the end of the month. Dad's tried everything, but it's no use. He's been given final notice to leave the site. There's nothing else we can do.'

'I don't suppose you know of anyone in Kilbarton who's looking for a second year apprentice mechanic, Gordon?' Tom asked glumly. He'd just started playing for the local football team, and didn't want to move.

'Sorry, Tom.' Gordon shook his head. 'I wish I could help. You know, I never knew John Elliot owned the business — I just took it for granted that it belonged to your dad.'

'Most people did,' Morag remarked. 'It didn't really make any difference, because Dad made all the decisions. No-one ever thought anything of it — until poor John died.'

Peggy nodded vigorously.

'And then it turns out that he's left everything to his nephew in Australia, who just sold the lot to developers, without saying a word!' she chipped in.

Gordon caught up with Morag as she walked down the path from the garage to the house. 'The garage finally closing — it's the end of an era,' he murmured. 'What will you all do?'

'I wish I knew.' Morag sighed. 'Mum's at the end of her tether, because right from the start Dad has refused to make any plans. He was so certain that we'd be able to stay here. It's only since we had word that the site would be cleared that he's accepted we'll have to leave.'

The full implication of her words made Gordon frown.

'So the house is going, too?' he asked.

Morag nodded, and allowed herself to pour out some of her worries, relieved she had someone to talk to about the situation.

She'd known Gordon for most of her life.

He'd been the one who taught her how to do small car repairs, when he worked as a mechanic with her father's business.

Then, when the engineering works closed, and he'd been paid off from the garage, he'd started a taxi business of his own. Now, at thirty, he owned a small fleet of taxis and had built up a good car rental business.

'By the way, I've decided not to go to the Red Cross Dinner Dance next month,' Morag told him suddenly. It was the one big annual function in Kilbarton, and for the last few years Morag and Gordon had gone together.

'Why ever not?' Gordon was unable to hide the disappointment in his voice. 'I thought you were looking forward to it.'

'I don't even know where I'll be living by then.' Morag shrugged. 'This way you've got plenty of time to find another partner.'

'Morag, Gordon!' a voice called.

They both turned to see Lorna Stewart hurrying across the garage forecourt towards them. Morag waved.

She and Lorna had been the best of friends since their schooldays.

'I've got your tickets for the dance,' Lorna said excitedly, rummaging in her bag.

'Lorna, I'm sorry, but I've decided not to go this year,' Morag told her. 'What with the garage closing . . . well, you know . . . '

'Oh, no!' Lorna wailed, looking at the bundle of unsold tickets in her hand.

Then she brightened.

'You'll still take the tickets, though, won't you, Gordon? And you don't need to worry about finding another partner — I'll go with you, if you like!' She batted her eyelashes theatrically at Gordon.

'I'll leave you two to sort it out — I'm going in for my breakfast.' Morag smiled.

Lorna was such a flirt, but she loved her friend dearly.

★ ★ ★

When Morag reached the kitchen her mother was standing very still at the sink, staring through the window.

'Hi, Mum. Is that my bacon under the grill?'

Helen Kinloch turned with a start. 'Sorry, love, I didn't hear you come in. Yes, it is. I've buttered some rolls for you, too.'

Morag sandwiched the crisp bacon in the rolls and sat down at the kitchen table. She'd manned the petrol pumps since before seven that morning, and she was hungry.

She saw her mother was still preoccupied.

It wasn't really surprising, she told herself. So many awful things were happening at the moment.

'Gordon's here — I've told him the news,' she told her mother. 'He says he'll do all he can to help.'

'That's kind of him,' Helen Kinloch said absently.

Morag lifted the morning paper and scanned it, trying to pretend she hadn't noticed her mother's odd behaviour.

But her heart was heavy . . .

They'd been such a happy, normal family till John Elliot's unexpected death. It didn't seem fair. He'd been content to leave the running of the business to her father — but when he died the Kinlochs discovered that his nephew in Australia had inherited everything.

There was no point in thinking like that, though, she told herself. We can't blame everything on John Elliot's death.

The business had thrived until the closure of the engineering works, which had employed almost a thousand men — that was the main culprit.

Now, they only just managed to scrape a living from the garage, with her father, Tom and herself running it, and Peggy and her mother in the shop.

Suddenly, her mother's voice broke into her thoughts.

'I got a letter from your Aunt Olivia this morning.'

Morag looked up, her breakfast suddenly forgotten.

'Aunt Olivia — Dad's sister? Why is she writing to you?'

Helen Kinloch took a crumpled envelope from her apron pocket.

'Here — read it yourself.'

Morag looked at the letter for a moment before opening it. Her father sometimes received letters from his sister, but he never read them.

Morag didn't know all the details, but she knew there was some kind of rift between them.

Simon and Olivia had argued years ago, and hadn't spoken since.

Morag slowly extracted the single handwritten page from its envelope and smoothed it out on the table.

Dear Helen, she read, *I have heard that Simon's business has been sold, and that you all have to leave your home. I'm finding it harder and harder to cope with things on my own, and I've decided to appoint a manager to ensure the continued smooth running of Herald Motors.*

I want to offer the job to Simon. I'd

also like to offer your family the top two floors of my home, for your exclusive use. My companion, Jemima, and I find the ground floor more than enough for our needs.

I want you to persuade Simon to take this position, although I realise I'm asking a great deal of you. I know now that I treated you very unfairly, but I've wanted to make peace for some years — to let bygones be bygones.

Please, Helen, try to find it in your heart to forgive me — Yours, Olivia.

Morag folded the letter and looked up at her mother. 'She wants Dad to manage Herald Motors?'

Though Morag had never met her aunt, she knew all about Olivia's business. It was one of the most prestigious car dealerships in Scotland, famous for its quality cars, especially its collection of vintage models.

'I just don't understand, Mum,' Morag said. 'Why would Aunt Olivia offer Dad a job now? I thought they hated each other. Didn't Dad once say that Olivia forced him to leave Herald Motors?'

Her mother sighed,

'It all happened a long time ago, love. After your grandfather died, Olivia decided she would take over as Managing Director. Your father objected, and after a lot of arguments Olivia managed to persuade the other directors to vote him off the board.

'The final straw came when she tried to stop your dad marrying me. I worked in the office at Herald Motors at the time, and I suppose Olivia felt I wasn't good enough to marry one of the Kinlochs.

'Anyway, your father felt he had no choice but to resign.' Helen Kinloch sat down wearily at the kitchen table.

'But why?' Morag persisted. 'Why did Aunt Olivia turn against Dad?'

'Olivia was seeing a man at that time,' Helen explained. 'Your dad's always thought this man encouraged Olivia to get rid of him — because he fancied the business for himself.

'He had no hope, though. Olivia's never believed that anyone could run Herald Motors as well as she does.' Helen's voice tailed off into gloomy silence.

'How do you think Dad will react?' Morag asked warily.

Helen shook her head.

'I just don't know. It's the best offer we've had, but there's so much at stake — and so much to forgive.'

Just then the door banged open, and Simon Kinloch walked in.

'Morning,' he said cheerily, but his smile faded as he recognised the handwriting on the letter Helen handed him.

For a moment, he was silent as he read the contents. Then he crushed the letter up in his fist and threw it to the floor.

'Good old Olivia!' His voice was heavy with sarcasm. 'She doesn't give up, does she? At long last she's seen her chance to get me under her thumb! Well, I'd rather starve!'

Helen stood up, slowly shaking her head. 'Simon, you can't dismiss it just like that. We need to talk about it. It's a good offer — in fact, it's the only one we've had.'

'No!' Simon Kinloch was adamant. 'Manager, indeed! I understand how Olivia's mind works. She'll expect us to be suitably grateful, and she won't let us forget how dependent we are on her.

'I had to take it when I was young, because she was fifteen years older than I was — but I'm not enduring it again now I'm nearer sixty than fifty!'

He turned quickly to Morag.

'I came in to ask a favour. Will you back Tom up on a repair delivery? It's an hour's drive and the car's wanted before lunch.' He pulled his wallet from his pocket and took out some notes.

'Here, the two of you deserve a break. Have a pub lunch somewhere.' Glancing once more at Helen, he went back out to the garage forecourt.

⋆ ⋆ ⋆

Morag and Tom set off half an hour later. Just before midday, they delivered the car to its owner and Tom took his place beside Morag in the small van she had followed in.

'Where are we going for lunch? I'm starving!'

'Here.' Morag pulled up outside a small hotel. 'The food's really good.'

Morag found a table while Tom went up to the bar to order some drinks. When he came back he was grinning.

'That barman recognised me!' he said excitedly. 'He saw me scoring my goal against Kiloran Rovers — the one that won the Amateur Cup.'

'You've scored one goal — and already you think you're a celebrity!' Morag laughed.

Getting a place in the local football team had been Tom's biggest ambition — and he could scarcely talk of anything else these days.

'Hello, you two!' Lorna Stewart's voice interrupted their laughter. 'Gordon, just look who's here. Surely this is a bit out of the way for you on a working day?'

Morag and Tom looked up and saw Lorna clinging to Gordon McEwan's arm.

'We've been on a delivery,' Tom explained, immediately launching into a detailed account of his winning goal to Lorna.

'Lorna and I are going to the dinner dance,' Gordon told Morag.

'Good idea!' She smiled brightly, yet she felt a pang of jealousy.

She'd no right to, she told herself sternly — she was the one who'd told Gordon to find another partner. Had she expected him to miss the dance simply because she didn't want to go?

Morag pushed her nagging thoughts aside.

Gordon was a good friend, nothing more — and if he wanted to take Lorna out, good luck to them.

Later, when Morag and Tom were driving back to the garage, he gave a wry laugh.

'Well, who would have thought it — Lorna and Gordon! Just shows you, doesn't it — she'd never have dreamed of going out with him before she got that fancy job in London — but now he's a businessman, not just a mechanic in some small-town garage.'

Morag didn't answer. She'd used to envy Lorna then, with her flat in London, her university degree and her busy social life. She'd seemed so happy, but then six months ago she'd given it all up and come back to Kilbarton.

Now she worked as an administrator at her father's busy medical practice.

Lorna had never revealed to Morag her reasons for leaving, but Morag had pieced together that her friend had suffered a painful broken romance.

For a long time Lorna had hidden the heartache behind the ever-cheerful front she kept up.

★ ★ ★

Later that evening, as the Kinlochs finished their meal, Gordon McEwan arrived.

'Come on in, Gordon,' Simon Kinloch said warmly. 'Will you have a cup of tea?'

'Yes, thanks.' Gordon found himself a seat in the cosy living-room.

'Look, I'll come straight to the point,' he began, looking round at Simon, Helen, Tom and Morag.

'You've all been so good to me over the years — treated me like one of the family. Well, now I want to return the favour.' He paused.

'My grandmother's old cottage is lying empty, and I'd like to offer it to you to live in,' he went on quietly.

'I could give Tom a job — he's a good mechanic. And Simon, if you're interested there's always a place for you as a taxi-driver. Maybe for the future we could think about a partnership in a used car business, too.'

Gordon looked round them quickly, trying to assess their reaction.

Morag saw the pulse beating in his temple and knew the effort it had taken for him to make the offer.

Gordon made no secret of how indebted he felt to her family, especially her father.

His parents had died when he was young and he'd been brought up by his grandmother.

When he'd left school with no qualifications and little prospect of a job, Simon had taken him in hand and given him an apprenticeship. And, although Gordon was now a business-man in his own right, her father was the one person he usually deferred to.

There was an uncomfortable silence in the room for a little, as the Kinlochs digested this offer.

Tom looked uneasily from one parent to the other, then turned his eyes appealingly to Morag.

'We'll leave you to discuss this,' Morag announced, getting up from the table. 'Tom and I have a repair that's wanted quickly.' She made for the door,

Tom at her heels.

'Thanks!' Tom mumbled as they walked up the path to the garage in the chill darkness. 'What do you think's going to happen?'

'I don't know, Tom. It's kind of Gordon to try to help, but . . . '

'But it's a bit of a comedown for Dad to work for one of his old apprentices,' Tom finished. 'I realise that. But what about you, Morag? What are you going to do?'

'I've been thinking about a computer studies course.' Morag's off-hand tone masked the anxiety she felt about the future. 'Or I might take Cathy up on her offer to stay at her flat in Glasgow.' She attempted a smile. 'That's what sisters are for, after all!'

'Looks like you've missed your chance there!' Tom joked.

'Whatever do you mean?' Morag asked in surprise.

Tom winked at her.

'One of Gordon's taxi-drivers knows a girl who teaches in the same school as

Cathy. She says our sister has a new flatmate — and he's male!'

Morag was about to tell him not to be so daft, then stopped. Her pretty younger sister had been strangely evasive recently. Her phone calls home were short and insubstantial, and she hadn't visited for a while.

In fact, the more Morag thought about it, the more plausible Tom's story seemed. She recalled that Cathy frequently mentioned Graham Bateman, a colleague of hers — was he the new flatmate? And if so, why hadn't Cathy told anyone about him?

'I'm sure Cathy will explain it all to us — if there is anything to explain,' she said cheerily, but her heart sank.

The last thing her parents needed right now was to worry about Cathy . . .

★ ★ ★

'Hi!' Gordon pushed open the garage door, putting an end to the conversation. 'I've been sent to bring you both

22

back in. Your mum and dad want to hear what you think before they make a final decision.'

'Oh, no!' Tom groaned. 'Can't they decide for themselves?'

Morag bit her lip.

'What do you think they're going to do, Gordon?'

He shrugged. 'As far as I can tell, they'd each like to make the other happy. Your mum seems to prefer the Herald Motors offer, although she's worried about sharing a house with your aunt.' He gave a rueful grin.

'I don't think your dad's at all happy about his sister's suggestion, though,' he finished quietly.

'Well, the only way to find out is to ask them!' Tom decided, making for the door.

Morag and Gordon followed him.

'Morag, what would you like to do now?' Gordon asked, as they wandered up the dimly-lit path to the house.

'Anything!' she replied. 'As long as

it's away from garages! I've had enough of petrol and grease and long hours!' She smiled.

'It's a shame my only skills are changing oil, filters and tyres, fitting windscreen wipers and headlamp bulbs! I'm not qualified to do anything other than work in a garage.'

'I never knew you hated the work here so much.' Gordon looked concerned, then ventured seriously, 'Morag, I . . . I was going to ask you . . . What I mean is, we get on really well together . . . '

'Oh, Gordon, please don't!' she interrupted. 'You don't have to make a job for me, too! You've done more than enough already.' She sighed.

'You asked me what I would like . . . ' Morag stopped. 'Look, Gordon, this isn't really the time to talk about this. Let's see what Mum and Dad have decided to do first.'

'OK,' he agreed. 'But just remember, Morag — I'm always here if you need someone to talk to.'

'Thanks, Gordon.' She smiled gratefully at him.

'Now let's go in and hear the verdict!'

'Come in — sit down!' Simon Kinloch gestured vaguely to the chairs grouped around the kitchen table.

'Your mum and I have decided that we can't make a decision about this family's future without letting you and Tom have a say, Morag.'

Morag gazed down at her hands, searching for the words to answer her father.

'It doesn't really affect me, Dad, because I've already decided to look for another job.'

She ignored her father's surprised expression and carried on.

'But since you've asked, I think you should consider Aunt Olivia's offer. You'd enjoy the job, and we wouldn't have to worry about finding a place to stay.' She looked into his anxious eyes.

'I know you're worried Aunt Olivia will interfere,' she pressed on, before her father could interrupt. 'If she does, you always have Gordon's offer to fall back on,' she pointed out.

'His cottage is big enough for you, Mum and Tom. I could always go and stay with Cathy and try to get a job in Glasgow.'

'I see.' Simon's face was expressionless. 'OK, Tom — let's hear what you have to say.'

Tom took a deep breath.

'What Morag said makes a lot of sense. Maybe it wouldn't be so bad, working for Herald Motors. And living in Glasgow might be fun.' He grinned. 'It could even improve my chances of playing for one of the big senior teams some day.'

He hung his head for a moment, then slowly admitted, 'But . . . I'd rather stay in Kilbarton.'

Helen Kinloch put her face in her hands for a moment, as her husband sighed.

'We're not much further forward, are we? Nobody seems to know what we should do.'

'Think things over,' Gordon suggested, getting to his feet. 'Take till the end of the week to decide — I'm in no great hurry for an answer.'

The Casting Vote

Hello — anyone home? It's just me!'
Cathy's voice sang out cheerfully as she
opened the front door of the bungalow.

In the kitchen Helen Kinloch's face
lit up.

Her younger daughter's arrival on
this frosty Saturday morning was an
unexpected surprise.

In moments Cathy was there, hugging her.

'What a lovely surprise!' Helen held
her daughter close.

'I got the chance of a lift from
Glasgow, so here I am! I wanted to find
out what's happening at first hand.'

'Nothing's been decided.' Helen
sighed.

Just then the kitchen door opened
and Tom's tousled head appeared.

He grinned when he saw his sister.

'Hi, Cath! Did you hear about my

winning goal in the cup final?'

'Yes — just a dozen times or so! I thought I might come along to the match later and give you some moral support.'

'Sure you can handle being the sister of a local celebrity?' Tom teased.

'Oh, I think I'll manage!' Cathy retorted, laughing at Tom's enthusiasm as he raced upstairs to get ready.

Helen smiled. 'Our problems come a poor second to Kilbarton Athletic as far as Tom's concerned — thank goodness. There's nothing he can do about it all — and his cheeriness is keeping us sane.

'But how are you, love? Everything OK at work . . . ?'

'Great! Great!' Cathy quickly changed the subject. 'Are you going to accept Aunt Olivia's offer?'

Helen shrugged. 'Your dad says he won't but he hasn't agreed to Gordon's offer, either. I'm sick to death of the whole thing. I just don't know what to do for the best.'

The back door opened and they both turned round expectantly as Morag rushed in to the kitchen.

In moments the two Kinloch sisters were hugging each other joyfully.

'Dad saw you getting out of the car and sent me down,' Morag said. 'It's been too long since we last saw you.'

'It certainly has,' Helen agreed. 'I'll put the kettle on.'

The three of them sat down at the kitchen table, and for ten non-stop minutes discussed all their news.

The conversation was lively, but Morag noticed that Cathy light heartedly evaded any questions about her new life in Glasgow.

She was more anxious to hear about the latest happenings in Kilbarton.

Helen Kinloch couldn't help comparing her two daughters as they chatted. She looked at them affectionately.

Morag, almost twenty-four years old, was the steady, reliable one.

Perhaps they'd expected too much of her — working garage shifts had meant she'd missed out on a lot of the things other girls simply took for granted.

As for twenty-two-year old Cathy — she always made Helen feel better. Her sunny nature and enthusiasm for life was a real treat.

'I'll come with you to see Dad,' Cathy decided as Morag got up to return to the garage.

The two sisters went out together, chattering, and Helen Kinloch felt a sudden lump rise in her throat.

It might be the last time she'd see them doing that, for in two weeks they had to leave this house, their home for over twenty years.

It was still unreal to her. And the rows and disagreements she and Simon were having depressed her.

They couldn't seem to see eye to eye about the future, and especially about Gordon's offer.

Helen liked Gordon McEwan, but she couldn't believe Simon would be happy working for him.

'Who gave you a lift here?' Morag

asked once they were away from the house. 'Was it Graham Bateman?'

'As a matter of fact it was,' Cathy replied cagily.

'I heard he was your new flatmate.'

'Oh! Well, yes . . . he is.'

'Isn't he married?' Morag asked.

When Cathy first started teaching, she'd occasionally mentioned Graham and his wife.

If he was married, Morag pondered, why had he moved into Cathy's flat?

Cathy stopped and turned to face Morag, a candid expression in her blue eyes as she answered her sister's question.

'He and his wife have split up, and he knew I was looking for someone to rent the spare bedroom in the flat. He asked me if I would mind letting him have it for a while,' she explained quietly.

'There's nothing going on, though,' she added quickly. 'We're just good friends.'

'I hope so,' Morag murmured, pulling open the door to the garage shop.

But Cathy didn't hear as she rushed inside to see her father.

'It does me good just to look at you!' Simon Kinloch told her warmly.

'She gets prettier every time I see her!' Peggy, the shop assistant, said.

Cathy had the grace to blush.

'No wonder Jamie Stewart is sweet on you, Cathy,' Peggy teased.

'Poor boy! Is he still hankering after a romance between us?' Cathy's laugh was off-hand.

Morag was saddened by Cathy's attitude, for until recently her sister had anxiously treasured any romantic overtures from Jamie, who was Lorna's brother.

Peggy's remark would have delighted her then.

Morag hoped fervently that Cathy's new flatmate wasn't the reason for her change of heart.

When Cathy mentioned that she was going to support Tom at the Kilbarton Athletic match that afternoon, Simon Kinloch turned to Morag.

'Why don't you go, too, love? Peggy and I can cope here.'

Simon walked to the door with his two daughters and stood on the empty forecourt with them — a tall, handsome, grey-haired figure.

Cathy asked about his plans for the future.

He shrugged.

'I think Gordon's offer has real potential. His idea is to combine the Kinloch family's garage expertise into a new business some time in the future.' His face shadowed as he went on.

'But I don't know if we could manage without Morag — and she's already made it clear she'd like to give up garage work.'

Morag immediately felt a pang of guilt, but it was soon replaced by annoyance. She'd sacrificed the chance of going to university and had worked in the garage for eight years. Surely she deserved a change?

Cathy was unimpressed with Simon's reasoning. 'Peggy could do the inside work just as well — answering tele-phones, taking bookings and so on,' she argued, looking sympathetically at Morag.

'Peggy's included in the offer — Gordon's asked her to work in his office when the garage closes,' Simon revealed.

★ ★ ★

An hour later the two sisters were standing on the narrow terracing of Kilbarton Football Club.

It was a crisp bright March day and Morag, after seeing Cathy's attractive outfit, had taken some time with her appearance. She'd decided to wear sleek black leggings with smart ankle-length boots and a huge, chunky chenille sweater.

Cathy had been impressed with her sister's appearance.

'You look great! Have you decided to change your image?' she'd asked.

Morag had laughed.

She'd forgotten how perceptive her young sister could be.

'It's about time, isn't it!' she'd replied lightly.

All thoughts of clothes were forgotten, however, as the teams ran on to the park and play began.

The game was lively and Tom played a significant part in the action, so the sisters were quite hoarse with cheering by half-time.

The players had just left the park when Gordon McEwan appeared.

'Like to come into the committee room for coffee?' he asked.

'We'd love to!' Cathy declared.

They went into the stone pavilion, built years ago when the town was prosperous.

Lorna Stewart was already inside, trying to sell tickets for the Red Cross Dinner Dance to the committee members.

'Hi, Morag, Cathy,' she greeted them. 'I'm not having much luck with these!'

She waved a bunch of unsold tickets.

'Morag, could I have a word — in private?' Lorna gestured to the door of a small office.

'OK,' Morag agreed with a smile.

The two girls went into the book-lined room and Lorna quickly closed the door behind them.

'I've heard from Max,' she said excitedly, holding out a letter. 'He's coming to Glasgow next week, and wants to see me. Read it!'

Lorna watched as Morag read the single page, anxious for her reaction. But Morag betrayed little as she raised her head.

'Is Max the man you left London to get away from?' she asked.

Lorna nodded.

'And are you going to phone him?' Morag asked.

'Do you think I should?'

Morag paused, sensing that Lorna desperately wanted her approval.

She handed back the letter.

'Lorna, I know how much he hurt

you before. But if you want to see him again, it's up to you. I suppose you could always agree just to meet him for lunch.'

'Lunch — of course!' Lorna's face lit up.

'That way you get to see him without the pressures of a dinner.'

Morag knew that, despite Lorna's feigned indifference, she wasn't interested in a trivial relationship.

'Maybe it would be best not to see him at all — that way there's no risk of being hurt again. But I suppose I'm just clinging to an outside chance that he's changed, and realised that I'm the only one for him!' Lorna finished with a sigh.

The door opened suddenly and Gordon McEwan looked in.

'Hurry up, you two — your coffee's getting cold.'

'We're just coming, Gordon — we were catching up on some gossip,' Lorna said brightly, ducking under his arm to leave.

'Some deep, dark secrets being revealed?' Gordon teased, as he and Morag suddenly found themselves alone in the narrow room.

'Lorna's ex-boyfriend from London is coming up to Glasgow next week and he wants to see her again,' Morag explained.

'Hope she knows what she's doing,' Gordon remarked. 'From what she's said about this Max, he seems to have treated her pretty badly.'

He turned slowly to face Morag.

'Look, have you thought any more about what you're doing to do?' he asked. 'Have you changed your mind about getting out of garage work?'

Morag was annoyed. Her father had been putting enough pressure on her without Gordon joining in, too.

'No. What made you think I might?' she asked coldly.

'I just wondered. You could always have a completely new career with me, you know. I'd really like to have you working with me.'

Morag stared at him, aware of something different about him.

True, she wasn't used to seeing him dressed like this, in a smart suit and tie. She was more used to seeing him in his working overalls, his face and hands smeared with oil.

'I want a change — it's as simple as that!' she said defensively. 'Now what about that coffee?'

'We could at least talk about it,' Gordon argued, standing his ground. 'How about having dinner with me, say Tuesday evening? I'll meet you at seven-thirty in the Brooklands Hotel.'

And without giving Morag the chance to refuse, he opened the door and ushered her out.

★　★　★

By Tuesday evening Morag was glad to get away from the house.

Over the weekend her parents had discussed endlessly the arguments for

40

and against both Gordon and Aunt Olivia's offers.

Morag was tired of being caught up in the middle of it all. Like her mother, she thought that Aunt Olivia's offer was their best option.

Her father was used to being his own boss, but if he took the job with Gordon McEwan, he would effectively be working for his one-time apprentice.

Knowing Simon's temperament, Morag was certain the reversal of roles wouldn't be a success.

Gordon arrived at the hotel just as she did, and they went in together.

Madge, the waitress, knew them both well and welcomed them with a cheery smile.

'Are you just having a bar supper — or is it a special candlelit dinner you're after?' she teased.

'Definitely dinner!' Gordon winked at her as, giggling, she bustled off to get the menu.

'You'd better watch what you're saying — she'll be telling half the town that we're going out together,' Morag remarked as she sat down.

'Maybe that's not such a bad idea!'

Morag glared at him.

She wasn't in the mood for Gordon's teasing.

She had so much on her mind at the moment, with her parents' situation, Cathy's new flatmate, Graham Bateman, and Lorna's ex-boyfriend, Max, coming back on the scene.

'You look lovely tonight,' Gordon said softly, his tone suddenly serious.

Morag was flattered, pleased that Gordon had noticed she'd taken extra care with her appearance for their evening out.

'Well, I thought I needed a change from greasy overalls! And I could say the same about you. This is the second time I've seen you in a suit recently!'

Gordon laughed, and Morag was struck by the difference it made to him.

He was usually so serious, completely dedicated to building up his business. Now that he looked relaxed and light hearted, he seemed like a completely different person.

Gordon finished his starter and pushed his plate away.

Then he fixed his gaze on Morag.

'Are you sure you want to change direction completely — career-wise, I mean? Or might you reconsider coming to work for me?'

It was the last thing Morag wanted to discuss.

She was tired of her father and Gordon trying to push her this way and that, when all she wanted was to decide for herself.

It was a relief when Madge came to remove their plates at that moment, but Gordon wouldn't let the subject drop.

As soon as Madge was out of earshot he started up again.

⋆　⋆　⋆

'I'm looking for some kind of long-term commitment, Morag,' he persisted, looking at her intently.

She was startled by Gordon's sincerity as their eyes met and held.

He'd offered her a job — but suddenly it seemed he was talking about more than just a working relationship . . .

'But what if your business fails in the end, too?' she argued. 'Dad was only just making enough for us to survive. Why should you do any better? And if that happened, I'd still be a semi-skilled dogsbody.' She sighed.

'All I want is to be qualified to do just one job — and have a bit of paper to prove it. Is that too much to ask?'

'No, it's not,' Gordon conceded, 'but once you've done your training — become a computer operator or whatever — then will you consider coming back to me?'

Morag didn't know what to say. There it was again — that hint of some kind of personal relationship in Gordon's words.

'You and I have always had a special relationship,' he pressed on, ignoring her confusion. 'And I know you'd have told me if there was someone else in your life. Don't you think it's about time we put things on a more serious footing?'

Morag suddenly felt she was being pressurised.

She was only twenty-four, and she was happy with the relaxed, friendly relationship she'd had so far with Gordon.

She wasn't ready to settle down yet — there was still too much she wanted to do with her life.

'Gordon, I don't know what to say. You've taken me completely by surprise. First you offer me a job — then you ask me to go out with you!'

'You know how I feel about you, Morag. I'd like us to make our relationship more permanent.'

'And what about what I want?' Morag demanded. 'I've had enough things to worry about lately without fretting about you and me! My parents are about to be made unemployed

— and homeless. My sister is sharing her flat with a married man. And Lorna . . . '

Morag broke off as she realised Gordon's attention had been distracted.

Instead, he was watching someone approaching their table from behind her.

'Hi! Fancy seeing you two here!' Lorna Stewart stopped at their table with a male companion. 'Max, these are my best friends, Morag and Gordon.'

There was a little flurry as introductory handshakes were exchanged.

Morag felt reprieved — Lorna's interruption was heaven sent. For the first time ever she'd felt out of her depth with Gordon.

'Do you mind if we join you?' Lorna asked suddenly. And, without waiting for a reply, she sat down at their table with Max. 'I've just been showing Max around the town,' she told them.

With Lorna and Max at the table there was no more time for serious discussion. Lorna chattered non-stop, and Morag found herself wishing that her friend would stop trying so hard to appear lively.

Max seemed quiet and shy, not at all like Morag had expected. She couldn't imagine him breaking any-one's heart . . .

'Max is going to be in Scotland for a few weeks and I've managed to persuade him to come to the dinner dance,' Lorna announced later on.

'Why don't we make it a foursome — I'm sure Max wouldn't mind partnering Morag,' Gordon said dryly. 'It would prove you can change your mind about something, Morag.'

Morag was furious.

Did Gordon think he could run her life?

First of all he'd decided that they should have a more serious relationship — now he was pressurising her into a date with a stranger.

'Oh, I can be very flexible when the occasion demands.' She smiled sweetly at Max. 'I'll make the effort for Lorna's sake, so she can sell another couple of tickets.'

And with that, she turned her back on Gordon and started chatting to Max about computer technology, a subject they were both interested in.

By the following Saturday morning Morag had simmered down. She even wished now she hadn't been so sharp with Gordon.

She really was very fond of him — she even hoped that some day they would get together. But not right now . . .

Cathy came home again that weekend, as the family's final decision on the future had to be taken.

★   ★   ★

The whole family sat down to lunch together on the Saturday, and Helen Kinloch swallowed her emotion as she watched them, thinking sadly that this would probably be one of the last meals they would take in this house as a family.

'I wonder where our next lunch together will be — in Granny Ewing's tiny kitchen, or under the lofty ceilings of Aunt Olivia's Edwardian town house?'

Cathy's casual remark brought tears to her mother's eyes, for it mirrored Helen's own thoughts.

None of them seemed to realise just how she would miss this house. The pain for her was like a bereavement.

This had been her first real home after she married Simon, and leaving it would be a wrench.

'Granny Ewing's kitchen could soon be enlarged. When we came here this house was very neglected, too,' Simon remarked.

'Yes.' Helen sighed. 'We started renovating room by room, till it was just the way we wanted it. And now it's all to go under a developer's bulldozer,' she said, with a tremor in her voice, which made them all look at her awkwardly.

Helen Kinloch was seldom emotional.

'I know what this place means to you — and to me, too,' Simon said quietly.

Helen gave him a shaky smile.

It was difficult for him, too — his life's achievements had just been swept away, through no fault of his own.

'There's no point in thinking like that,' Cathy said brightly. 'It's the future you have to think about now. You've got to decide which option to go for — join Gordon, or become Aunt Olivia's manager.'

Helen looked at her younger daughter. It all seemed so simple to her. The glaring pitfalls in both these alternatives meant nothing to Cathy.

'This steak pie, Mum — it's one of your best!' Tom said, shovelling more on to his plate.

He hated these protracted discussions, and preferred to ignore them.

He just wished everything would stay the same, although becoming a mechanic with Gordon would not be too much of a change.

And, once his father and Gordon got

the repair and second-hand car business going, life wouldn't be much different to now — and they would still live in Kilbarton.

Suddenly, the front door bell rang, and they all looked at one another.

Only strangers used the front door . . .

Simon got up, frowning.

In the kitchen there was silence, then surprise, as they heard his voice at the door, welcoming someone.

'Come in, Michael. Great to see you! It's been years!'

They heard the lounge door opening, and the stranger being ushered in.

'Helen, come and see an old friend,' Simon called through to the kitchen.

Morag, Cathy and Tom ate the rest of their lunch on their own, aware of the voices through in the lounge.

Almost without realising, they strained to hear what was being said.

Despite their father's seeming good humour, they were anxious. Strange visitors seemed to bring trouble these days.

Cathy was the first to break the silence.

'Morag, let's see all these new clothes you've been buying,' she suggested.

'Go ahead, don't mind me.' Tom grinned good-naturedly. 'Clothes don't interest me at all.'

The two sisters went through to Morag's bedroom.

Cathy was impressed at how she had almost doubled her wardrobe in the last few weeks.

'I can't wear jeans and jumpers to job interviews.' Morag smiled, and added quietly, 'Any chance of staying in your spare room if I'm stuck?'

Cathy stiffened.

'I suppose so . . . in a few weeks. I can't just throw Graham out. It's been such a traumatic time for him.'

'Doesn't he have parents or relations he could stay with?'

'He doesn't want them to get dragged into the break-up of his marriage. It's been pretty messy.'

'But he's staying with you — that drags you into it!' Morag pointed out.

'No, it doesn't! I'm not involved — he's just my flatmate.'

'Cathy, you know Mum and Dad wouldn't like it.'

'I know,' Cathy conceded. 'You're not going to tell them, are you?'

'No — but someone else might,' Morag pointed out quietly. 'And you know how people around here gossip . . . '

'Well, let them!' Cathy snapped, hurrying out of the room.

Morag's blunt questions had ruffled her and made her uncomfortable.

She hadn't thought of the complications when Graham Bateman first asked if he could move into the spare bedroom in her flat.

He seemed so exciting and mature, and it was flattering to be considered a friend by such a senior member of the teaching staff.

★   ★   ★

Simon and Helen Kinloch stared at their visitor, who had just told them his reason for coming — to beg Simon to accept Olivia's offer of managing Herald Motors.

'We need someone to run the place now Olivia's house-bound. Day by day the business is failing in front of my eyes.'

Michael McQuade, chief mechanic at Herald Motors, gazed back at them, concern etched on his honest, middle-aged face.

'Olivia didn't mention anything about the firm being in trouble.' Simon frowned.

Michael McQuade's sudden appearance had perturbed him.

It took him back through the years to when he and Helen had decided to get married.

Michael had been a good friend to them, and he'd cheerfully risked Olivia's anger by helping them, although he was Herald Motors' chief mechanic even then.

'I don't think she realises how bad things have got. But I can tell, just by looking round at the stock. I don't know where to start.' Michael shook his head helplessly. 'I'm just a mechanic . . . '

'Has Olivia put you up to this?' Simon's tone was harsh. 'Did she send you?'

Michael looked bewildered and hurt by Simon's hostility.

'No, she doesn't know I've come — I didn't decide myself until this morning. I overheard one of my best mechanics talking about looking for another job because he thinks Herald Motors is on the way down.

'It made me realise I'm not the only one who's been noticing things . . . '

Michael's voice tailed away miserably, and he sat, head bowed, examining his hands.

Helen Kinloch longed to go and put a comforting arm round his shoulder.

She looked over at her husband and faltered a little, for he was silently appealing to her for help.

But this was one thing Simon had to decide for himself.

He knew what she thought — she'd

told him often enough in the last few weeks that she believed Olivia's offer was the better of the two.

'Mechanics didn't leave Herald Motors in my day,' Simon remarked after a while.

'And this is the first time I've ever known it to happen,' Michael retorted. 'Simon, something's going on at Herald Motors and Olivia isn't around to sort it out. I'll be out of a job if you don't take over — and quick!'

At this direct appeal Simon Kinloch floundered a little.

He was always willing to help wherever he could — but to go back and work for his sister, after all that had happened between them?

He turned away, frowning.

'Look, if Olivia could turn the clock back she would. She knows she was in the wrong, even though she could never bring herself to apologise.' Michael's tone was blunt, his gaze appealing. 'But blood's thicker than water, and she's asking for help now — and so am I. Just give me a straight answer — yes, or no!'

'We can't give an answer here and now,' Helen said calmly. 'We'll have to discuss it with the rest of the family.'

Michael shrugged resignedly.

'Fair enough.'

'I'll ask them to come in then.' Simon went to the door, opened it and called, 'Morag! Cathy! Tom! — come through here, please.'

Once the family had assembled, Simon introduced their visitor.

'I've come to try to persuade your father to accept the job at Herald Motors. We really need him there,' Michael McQuade said bluntly.

'Your mother and I didn't want to make a decision without letting you all have your say,' Simon explained. 'Michael, you'd better tell them what you've just told us.'

Ten minutes later, Morag found everyone looking at her.

'Morag, it looks as if you've got the casting vote,' her father said. 'Your mother and Cathy both think we should accept Olivia's offer. Tom and I would rather work for Gordon. What do you want to do?'

'Dad, I can't decide for you — it's up to you and Mum,' Morag said, alarmed at the responsibility she was being given.

'Please, just tell us what you think, love.' Simon Kinloch looked tired and drained. 'Your mother feels the only fair way to settle this is to accept the majority decision.'

'OK.' Morag bit her lip. 'I agree with Mum and Cathy. I think Aunt Olivia's offer is best.'

Simon Kinloch took a deep breath, curbing his annoyance. Then he nodded his head several times as if conceding defeat.

'Well, that's it then, Michael, you can tell Olivia I'll start a week on Monday.'

Then he turned almost sorrowfully to Morag.

'I never thought that you, of all people, would let Gordon McEwan down so badly.'

On the Move

Take the next turning on the right,' Helen Kinloch told Gordon. He steered the large white car into the private road of dignified Edwardian houses, edging past the carefully-tended lawns.

The car drew to a halt outside number seven.

'It hasn't changed a bit!' Helen sighed, looking up at the handsome Edwardian façade. 'They're even the same curtains — and I remember those lace-edged blinds with tassels!'

'It's just nine-thirty — are we too early?' Gordon asked, turning to Morag in the back seat.

It was Helen who answered him.

'No, Olivia said just to come whenever it was most convenient for us. She's expecting us.'

Morag sat on, suddenly reluctant to get out and walk up the wide stone steps to the front door and meet this aunt, whom she'd heard so much about.

Helen roused herself.

'There's no point in waiting around out here. Let's get it over with and find out what Olivia has to say.'

She put a hand on Gordon McEwan's arm.

'Thanks for driving us through. It was really good of you.'

'No problem! Just give me a call when you want a lift back.'

'Thanks, Gordon.' Helen Kinloch smiled gratefully at him as Morag helped her out of the car.

They waited on the pavement until Gordon drove away.

Morag had been quiet for most of the journey. Gordon's offer of a lift had been really helpful, yet somehow it irritated her.

She didn't know where she stood with him now. He seemed to have changed recently.

He'd become strangely confident in

the last few weeks, where before he'd been quite retiring, never pushing himself forward.

She followed her mother up the steps of the house and rang the bell.

A thin, elderly woman opened the door, and looked up at Helen.

'It's good to see you again, Mrs Kinloch. Come in, please.'

'Good morning, Jemima!' Helen said briskly. 'This is my elder daughter, Morag. Morag, this is Jemima, your Aunt Olivia's companion and house-keeper.'

Morag pulled back slightly as the old woman peered into her face.

'You've got your father's height, and your mother's colouring,' she announced after a moment, then slowly started to climb the four steps behind her that led to the hall.

She turned halfway up and saw them waiting on the doorstep.

'Come on — this way! I'm too old to stand on ceremony. And close the door behind you.'

They followed her into the dark house, and were soon shown into a large room off the hall, which Morag guessed was the dining-room. But the table was pushed against the wall opposite the fireplace, and a divan bed had been placed underneath the window.

'Come in, I'm glad you agreed to see me.'

The voice came from behind a large winged chair which faced the blazing coal fire.

Helen Kinloch took the initiative and walked straight up to the chair. Her voice was wintry.

'Good morning, Miss Kinloch — '

'Hello, Helen. So this is your daughter, Morag.' Olivia cut in, a wisp of a smile softening her face as she looked at her niece for the first time. 'My hearing is still acute, even if the rest of me is a mess — arthritis has taken its toll on me, I'm afraid. Come in, please, and sit down!'

The tall figure sitting upright in the chair, supported by cushions, impressed

Morag — especially her hair, which was carefully styled.

'My hairdresser comes once a week,' Olivia said, as if answering her unspoken query. 'We've a daily each morning to keep the place tidy, and Jemima does the cooking. Two old women like us don't eat much anyway! So it's just the two of us in this enormous house.'

Olivia Kinloch gazed steadily at the two women before her, noting the stiff suspicion on her sister-in-law's face.

'I agreed to come here today to find out exactly what your offer entails.' Helen tried to sound businesslike, but her voice shook.

She was appalled at the toll the years had taken on Olivia. It was unbelievable that the tall, perfectly-dressed woman she remembered had been brought to this.

'I'll pay Simon twenty-five per cent. more than he earns now. He'll have full control of Herald Motors, without any interference from me. You'll also have the two floors above this one for your own use, rent free.'

Olivia Kinloch lifted an envelope from the small table beside her and held it out to Helen.

'My lawyer has drawn up this agreement giving you both uncondi-tional tenancy. Even if Simon finds he can't work with me, you'll still have somewhere to live.'

Helen opened the envelope and examined the document.

She deliberately took much longer than she needed in order to mask her confusion — all the questions she'd wanted to ask had already been answered without argument!

⋆　⋆　⋆

'Would you like to see the rooms upstairs?' Jemima asked, breaking the silence.

She got to her feet and looked expectantly at Helen and Morag.

'Helen, would you mind staying down here with me?' Olivia Kinloch said. 'Morag can look first. You and I have a lot of years to catch up on.'

Morag glanced at her mother, who nodded to her to go. Then she followed Jemima out of the room and up the wide staircase, where a deep red carpet, anchored with broad brass rods, covered the dark oak treads.

Jemima stopped on the landing under a long, stained-glass window to recover her breath.

She took the opportunity to study Morag closely, then shook her head.

'Imagine Simon having a daughter your age! I brought him up, you know,' she confided as she climbed the next flight of steps. 'You probably know the story,' she went on. 'His mother died soon after he was born. I was just twenty then, so he was like my own child.

'He never came to see me after he married your mother, though. Of course, at the time, I agreed with Olivia — we thought he was too young to take on the responsibilities of marriage as well as a career.'

She shook her head, almost in wonder.

'But we were wrong!'

Down in the dining-room, Helen sat on the edge of the sofa, aware that Olivia Kinloch was watching her closely.

'For nearly two years now this room has been my world,' Olivia told her. 'My bed is over there by the window, the phone here on my left, and my dining-table and desk is this adjustable top, which fits over my lap.' She indicated it to the right of her chair.

'I can't walk now, you see,' she said bluntly.

'It must have been very difficult for you to come to terms with,' Helen said with careful politeness.

'I've got used to it.' Olivia shrugged. She looked at Helen intently.

'I take it Simon still doubts my motives,' she said abruptly, changing the subject. 'After all, he's declined to come here with you.'

Helen paused before answering.

She was wary of this woman, but she felt instinctively that a little straight talking might clear the air.

'Simon has had two job offers — yours, and one from Gordon McEwan, a family friend who owns a taxi business in Kilbarton,' she explained.

'Gordon's offer would mean Simon working for his former apprentice, and I don't think he would take kindly to that — he's too used to making the decisions himself. For that reason, and because we have no other option, I want him to take the job with Herald Motors.'

'I see!' Olivia was brisk.

Before she could say any more, the door opened and Jemima and Morag came into the room.

'What do you think of the accommodation?' Olivia Kinloch asked.

'It's certainly spacious!' Morag admitted. 'There's some lovely furniture up there.'

'Come and I'll show you round.' Jemima beckoned to Helen.

'Let me know what you want changed about before you move in, and where you want your furniture placed,' Olivia offered as Helen rose to follow Jemima. 'And now I'll get to know my niece.'

Morag sat down, facing Olivia again.

'This break-up of the business is very difficult for you — it leaves you out of a job, doesn't it?' Olivia Kinloch said sympathetically.

'It's not good.' Morag tried to keep the bitterness out of her voice.

She told her aunt ruefully of how she'd given up her chance to go to university in order to work for the family business.

Now, eight years later, it seemed her sacrifice had been for nothing.

Olivia nodded sympathetically.

'It can't have been easy.'

'No,' Morag conceded. 'Anyway, now I've decided to do something completely different. I want to get some proper training — in computers, maybe. I've had enough of oil-stained hands!' She laughed lightly.

Olivia looked closely at her niece.

'I've had an idea. I have some business interests in the fashion trade. There's a vacancy that might appeal to you until you find what you want — assistant in a wedding gown showroom. One of the girls has just gone off on maternity leave.'

The offer was so unexpected that for a moment Morag was speechless.

'When . . . ?' she managed to ask.

'As soon as possible. You could go today and speak to the acting manageress if you like.' Olivia Kinloch indicated the phone at her elbow. 'I can arrange it now.'

Morag smiled gratefully.

'That's very good of you. I'd love to go. It sounds the complete opposite of what I've been doing lately.'

Olivia suddenly smiled back at her and lifted the phone.

After a short conversation, she turned to Morag.

'It's all arranged. And, since it's

raining, Lorraine, the acting manager-ess, will come here to collect you.'

'Thank you so much!' Morag laughed, suddenly light-hearted at getting a job interview with such ease.

In a way it seemed to lift the sense of foreboding which had haunted her since the sale of the garage.

'Tell me about Tom, Morag,' Olivia said, changing the subject. 'Will he continue his apprenticeship with Herald Motors? I know he plays for the local football team in Kilbarton, so maybe there's a chance he'll want to stay there?'

'I think he'll come here — I can't see him fending for himself without Mum's home cooking!' Morag replied.

Just then a car drew up outside, and in a moment a smartly-dressed young woman was peeping round the door of Olivia's room.

'Come in, Lorraine — this is Morag, my niece. I'd like you to take her to the shop and show her what's involved in the wedding gown trade.'

'Pleased to meet you.' Lorraine shook Morag's hand, then stood back to look at her.

Morag shifted awkwardly, a little uncomfortable at Lorraine's scrutiny.

'Oh, I'm sorry for staring!' Lorraine apologised. 'I was just thinking how good it is that you're tall. Sometimes our customers like to see someone modelling the dresses — it helps them to choose. Your height will show the gowns off perfectly.'

Morag felt a little thrill of excitement as Lorraine started the car, but then gasped in surprise.

Gordon's white limousine was parked just outside the gates and he was sitting behind the wheel, reading a paper. He looked up and saw them, and wound down his window.

'Friend of yours?' Lorraine asked, slowing down.

'Yes, he is. He drove us here this morning.'

'He looks gorgeous! Is he your boyfriend?'

'Well . . . not really. We're just good friends.'

Morag found it difficult to describe their relationship now, especially since Gordon had told her he wanted to make things more permanent between them.

She wound down her window as Lorraine stopped the car beside Gordon's.

'My appointment didn't take as long as I expected. I'm ready to leave when you are — just give me a call.' He pointed to the car phone on the dashboard.

'You can have my number any time!' Lorraine smiled flirtatiously, starting to drive off.

Morag frowned a little at the other girl's behaviour.

She hadn't realised that other women found Gordon McEwan so attractive, but Lorraine obviously did — and Lorna had flirted with him, too.

★   ★   ★

The smile on Helen Kinloch's face faded when she came back into the room with Jemima.

'Where's Morag?' she demanded.

'I've fixed up a job interview for her,' Olivia said. 'It's at a local bridal salon. She'll be back soon.'

Helen swallowed, suddenly recalling her husband's vehement assertion that his elder sister would take over their lives, given the chance.

But she pushed it away — Morag was no fool, she reminded herself.

And in a short time Morag was back.

'It just couldn't be a bigger contrast to working in the garage,' she told her mother excitedly. 'The salon's so luxurious!'

'Do you think you'd enjoy learning to manage such a business?' Olivia Kinloch asked quietly.

Morag looked at her intently.

'Manage? I thought I was being offered the assistant's job?'

'Yes, but only for a few weeks. Hopefully, you'd soon have enough experience to take over as manager. Lorraine is a good saleswoman and has a flair for buying, but she's not responsible enough to manage the business permanently.'

'It sounds very tempting,' Morag said reflectively. 'But I don't know if I'd be any good at it — I never had to sell anything in the garage.'

'You didn't need to. The customers knew you gave first-class service and value for money. That's proper selling!' Olivia said firmly.

'Well, I'll try — and if I don't think it's working out, I'll tell you.' Morag was frank.

'Don't worry, you're a Kinloch. You'll succeed!' Olivia was confident.

Morag and Helen hadn't noticed Jemima leaving the room, so it surprised them when she pushed in a heavily-laden trolley.

'Jemima will be insulted if you don't stay for some lunch,' Olivia said.

Morag and Helen exchanged glances.

'Gordon McEwan is waiting outside,'

Helen murmured.

'Go and bring him in — there's plenty!' Jemima waved her hand proudly over the spread.

Soon Gordon was sitting with them sharing, with obvious enjoyment, the excellent hot quiches and salads.

He spoke with easy authority to Olivia about general garage business. And, watching him, listening to him, Morag suddenly wondered if she had ever really known Gordon.

He seemed so very different . . .

The last-minute arrangements were finished and it was mid-afternoon when they left.

'Do you think we might pop in to the flat to see Cathy? School will soon be over,' Helen suggested.

'Oh, no! It . . . It's too early yet . . . and Gordon has to get back.'

Morag was quick to squash the idea. The last thing she wanted was for her mother to discover who Cathy's new flatmate was.

'Yes. I've got a few bookings for

tonight,' Gordon said, backing Morag up, and she relaxed. Her mother wouldn't pursue the idea now.

They made the return journey in near silence, each coping with their own thoughts of the day.

Helen Kinloch sighed deeply as they neared home.

'I've a hunch that arranging things with Olivia might be the easiest part of the move. Your father's still not convinced we've made the right choice.'

When the car drew up at the garage, she got out quickly. She called her thanks to Gordon, and hurried into the bungalow.

Morag lingered a little, putting off going into the house. She knew her father wouldn't be enthusiastic about the plans for the move, and she was too tired to listen to all the old arguments being repeated.

Gordon turned to her in the back seat and regarded her intently.

'Why did you choose Olivia's offer and not mine?' he asked.

'Isn't it obvious? Dad would have been working for you — his old apprentice. It would have ended in tears!' She was deliberately flippant.

He looked at her for a seemingly endless moment, then nodded.

'That's more or less what your mother said, too,' he commented.

Morag got out of the car, then turned back to try to explain further.

'There's another reason for accepting Olivia's offer. Anything that might end the feud between her and Dad can only be good,' she said quietly.

He sat in the car and looked up at her. 'It would have worked, you know. Your father and I considered that, in five to ten years, we could have built a business to rival Herald Motors.'

He gave her a small, wry smile and drove off.

Morag realised then that she'd hurt Gordon by preferring the Herald Motors' offer, and she was sorry. But in her heart she knew that Gordon's plan would never have worked.

★ ★ ★

The next few days were hectic, as the whole family packed the furniture and contents of their home, ready for the move to Glasgow.

Simon Kinloch became quieter and more tense as the day of the move approached.

'Simon, please try to be more positive about the future,' Helen pleaded on their last evening in the bungalow. 'I know you're sceptical about Olivia's motives, but you'll have a job — and we'll all have somewhere to live. A few weeks ago it looked as though we'd have neither of those.'

'I know, love.' Simon sighed. 'I should be grateful.'

'And remember, too, that Michael McQuade's on your side. He says Herald Motors needs you,' Helen went on, 'Olivia simply can't afford to drive you away again.'

'You're right,' Simon agreed. 'But leaving this place is such a wrench

— it's the end of an era. All those years of hard work seem wasted now — in the end they just weren't enough.'

'I feel that way, too,' Helen murmured, laying a hand on her husband's arm. 'But there's no point in looking back — that won't change anything. We have to make the most of this new chance.'

Simon smiled gratefully at his wife, pulling her close. He knew how hard all this was for Helen, and he admired her strength. If only he could display the same confidence in the future.

Footsteps on the path outside made them both jump.

'It's only Morag,' Simon said, peering out into the darkness. 'Oh, and Lorna's with her.'

He pulled open the back door and the two girls rushed in, rubbing their cold hands.

'Morag and I have just done a deal for the Red Cross fête,' Lorna said excitedly. 'I've bought the remainder of your confectionery stock.'

'The boxes are in my room.' Morag led the way along to her bedroom, where a row of brightly-coloured boxes lined the wall.

Lorna closed the door behind them and looked at Morag.

'Can we talk?' she asked.

'What is it now?' Morag shook her head in amused exasperation. Lorna always made such a crisis out of everything that happened to her.

'Please, Morag — you have to come to the cheese and wine party on Sunday night. Gordon says he'll go if you do. And it would be nice if Max could see a few familiar faces. You two seemed to get on well together.'

'But we'll just be settling into the new house then. There'll probably be loads of unpacking to do . . . '

'That can wait, surely. Oh, please, Morag!' she pleaded. 'It'll only be for a few hours. I'd really like you to be there.'

Morag thought for a moment.

She knew how excited and flattered

Lorna felt at having Max back in her life. But she also knew how afraid her friend was of being hurt again by him.

It was obvious to Morag that Lorna wanted her to go to the party to provide a little moral support.

'OK, I'll go!' Morag decided.

'Oh, thanks, Morag! I'll do the same for you one day, I promise!'

★   ★   ★

Saturday, the day of the removal, was grey and damp — a reflection of how I feel, Helen Kinloch thought sadly, at leaving this house behind. Cathy arrived early from Glasgow to help and she, too, seemed downcast.

Only Tom was cheerful, but then, Saturdays meant just one thing to him — football.

Today was no different, in spite of the move.

He rushed into the kitchen, where Helen was busy packing the last of the kitchen cutlery into a box.

'Wish me luck, Mum!' he greeted her. 'It's the final of the Kilbarton and District Cup today!'

Helen turned to him, smiling at his youthful exuberance.

'I hope you get a hat-trick!'

'I'd settle for the winning goal!' He grinned, giving her a hug, then hurried out.

'It's a pity we couldn't go to the match today, Cathy,' Morag said, watching Tom from her bedroom window. 'It would have meant a lot to Tom to have some of the family to cheer him on.'

Cathy didn't reply as she half-heartedly sorted through the chest of drawers, and her sister looked at her anxiously.

'What is it, Cath? You seem really down today.'

Cathy shook her head helplessly, finding it difficult to express her feelings. 'Oh, Morag, I'm in such a mess. Graham seems to have got the wrong idea completely,' she said quietly.

'He's talking about divorcing his wife, so that we can get married.'

'Is that what you want?'

'No! When I offered him the spare room, it was as a flatmate — nothing more. But he's putting a lot of pressure on me to get involved with him,' Cathy revealed. 'It's a bit scary.'

Morag sighed, remembering the misgivings she had felt originally.

She'd tried to warn Cathy of the dangers of taking Graham Bateman in, but her sister had refused to listen.

'I suppose you could give up your flat and come to live at Aunt Olivia's,' Morag suggested.

'But I can't just kick Graham out! He's got nowhere else to go!' Cathy protested.

'Then give him the rent book, and let him find someone to take the spare bedroom,' Morag said.

'I could, couldn't I? I never thought of that,' Cathy said hopefully.

Then her eyes filled with tears.

'I should have listened to you,

Morag,' she murmured. 'You told me I was making a mistake . . . '

'Well, there's no use thinking of what you should have done,' Morag said briskly. 'Just make sure things don't get any worse!'

She smiled at her sister.

'Why don't you finish off here while I go and help Mum in the kitchen?'

Downstairs, as she helped empty the kitchen cupboards, Morag stiffened when her mother suddenly asked, 'Is Cathy worried about something?'

'What do you mean?' Morag turned away, unwilling either to deceive her mother or betray her sister's confidence.

'I don't know, exactly. She just doesn't seem herself.' Helen Kinloch sighed. 'Maybe she's upset about the move, too.'

Morag nodded, relieved she hadn't had to lie to her mother and giving her cause for concern. Helen had so much to worry about already without being told that Cathy was involved with a married man.

Three hours later, the final box was loaded into the removal van, which set off for Glasgow.

The bungalow was stripped bare and, as the Kinlochs wandered from room to room, their voices echoed.

All they had to do now was wait for Tom to come home from the football match. Then they, too, could leave for Glasgow.

'What's keeping him?' Simon Kinloch said impatiently, after they'd been waiting for almost an hour.

'Gordon said he'd drive Tom home immediately after the game,' Helen pointed out. 'They must have been held up.'

'Here's a car — but it's Lorna's!' Morag watched, puzzled, as an ashen-faced Lorna ran towards the back door.

'It's Tom — he's been hurt! They're taking him to the hospital in Glasgow,' Lorna blurted out, stumbling into the kitchen.

'What's happened? Is he OK?' Simon demanded.

'He's been taken by ambulance to

the Royal Infirmary. His leg is broken, and they think he may have fractured his skull.'

Lorna's voice trembled.

'Oh, it should never have happened! He'd just scored the winning goal, but he slipped and collided with the goalpost.'

'Oh, no!' Helen gasped, clutching for Simon's arm. 'We have to go to him, Simon.'

She started to sob softly as her husband put his arm around her.

'Gordon's gone in the ambulance with him,' Lorna went on. 'He asked if one of you would be prepared to take his car through to Glasgow, so he can get home later.'

'I'll drive it,' Morag offered at once.

'And I'll keep you company,' Cathy added quickly.

'That's settled, then,' Simon announced. 'Let's get there as quickly as we possibly can.'

He shepherded them out without a backward glance at the bungalow and drove off in the direction of Glasgow.

Lorna Stewart looked sadly at Morag and Cathy.

'I'm sure Tom will be fine,' she said, trying to reassure them. 'He's young and healthy — he'll bounce back.'

The sisters nodded, hoping with all their hearts it was true.

I Don't Like
That Man . . .

Simon Kinloch drove the few miles from the hospital to Olivia's home in silence, his white-knuckled hands gripping the steering-wheel the only sign of tension.

Helen sat beside him in the passenger seat, staring straight ahead.

As the car turned into the tree-lined road where Olivia lived, Helen broke the silence.

'I hated leaving Tom there — he looked so helpless.'

'I know, love.' Simon sighed. 'But you heard what the doctor said — Tom needs to rest. There was no point in us waiting around at the hospital — especially when there's so much to see to here.'

He stopped the car and gestured to

the imposing Edwardian house in front of them.

'After the trouble Olivia caused for us before we were married, I swore I'd never return here. Well, look at me now,' he said bitterly. 'What a failure! After twenty-five years away, I'm back where I started, working for Olivia again.'

He gazed despondently out of the car window, and Helen realised that, just then, he felt he'd lost control of his life.

The business he'd built up so painstakingly had been wiped out, and the rest of the family had urged him to take a job he didn't really want.

He must be feeling anxious, too, about meeting Olivia again . . .

'A failure? Rubbish!' Helen said sharply. 'Having to close the business wasn't your fault — it was out of your control. And Olivia wouldn't have given you this job unless she knew you were up to it. Herald Motors is her livelihood — she can't afford to make mistakes with it.'

'You're right!' Simon clasped her hand tightly in his. 'Let's go inside and get this over with.'

They hurried up the steps to the front door, which opened as they approached.

Jemima, Olivia Kinloch's house-keeper and companion, came forward to welcome them.

'Simon! It's so good to see you again,' the old woman said. 'Oh, it's been too long! Come away in, both of you.'

Just then a taxi pulled up at the front door and Gordon McEwan got out. He'd met Simon and Helen at the hospital, and they'd invited him back to Olivia's house.

'Hello, Gordon,' Jemima greeted him warmly.

The three of them followed her into the old dining-room, where Olivia was sitting by the fire.

When she saw Simon, Olivia tried to stand.

He paused at the door, shaken by the sight of her.

Helen had warned him that the years had taken their toll on his elder sister, but he'd been unprepared for the extent of the change.

'It's been too long, Simon,' Olivia murmured hoarsely, sinking back into the cushions of her chair.

Simon went slowly over to her and took her hand.

Helen watched, knowing that she could never like Olivia, but that she truly wanted these two to bury their grudges.

Twenty-five years was long enough — and Olivia wanted to make peace. It was only right they should meet her halfway.

'Yes, we've a lot of years to make up for,' Simon said. 'I hope we can put the past behind us and make this work.'

'I do, too,' Olivia said candidly. 'But first of all — how's Tom? Morag rang and told me that you'd both gone straight to the hospital.'

'The doctor says he's as well as can be expected,' Simon told Olivia, laying a comforting hand on Helen's shoulder.

'He's broken his leg, but it's been set.' For his wife's sake he tried to speak calmly.

'He'd regained consciousness by the time we reached the hospital, so we were able to speak to him. The doctors want to keep him in overnight, though, for observation. He did have concussion, you see.'

'The doctor told us that what Tom needs now is rest,' Helen added, noting the real concern in Olivia's eyes and appreciating the older woman's quiet sympathy. 'That's why we came back here — there didn't seem any point in waiting at the hospital for hours while Tom slept. We're going back to visit him this evening.'

'I wish I could say, or do, something to help,' Olivia said.

'Some tea — that's what we need,' Jemima announced briskly. 'And some food, too. I'll fetch a tray.'

She bustled off to the kitchen and returned a few minutes later with a laden tray.

'Food — Jemima's answer in every situation.' Olivia Kinloch smiled. 'And it always helps, doesn't it?'

Helen looked at the apple tart, buttered scones and fruit loaf on the table, all baked by Jemima. They were all Simon's long-time favourites, and she was touched that the old woman had gone to so much trouble to prepare for their arrival.

And, as cups and plates were passed round, she realised that Olivia was right. Sharing food broke down tensions and created a bond.

Soon, Olivia and Simon were discussing his new job at Herald Motors, albeit with some reserve.

Helen took the opportunity to thank Gordon McEwan for travelling to the hospital with Tom in the ambulance.

'You're a good friend, Gordon,' she said gratefully, looking at him with a smile. She marvelled at how much he'd changed in the fifteen years she'd known him.

When Simon first took him on as an

apprentice, she'd wondered if he was doing the right thing — Gordon had seemed so difficult and unfriendly then.

But he'd applied himself to the job and worked harder than any apprentice they'd had before, and gradually he learned to trust them, in time becoming almost one of the family.

She sometimes wondered if he and Morag would end up together — they'd always been close, but lately Morag had seemed to be growing away from them all . . .

★　★　★

Morag and Cathy set off from Kilbarton shortly after their parents.

Lorna Stewart had driven them to pick up Gordon's car from his garage, as he'd asked.

She had been able to tell the sisters very little about the extent of Tom's injuries, and Morag could think of nothing else as she drove to their new home in her aunt's house.

Cathy, however, was still preoccupied with the problems her flatmate, Graham Bateman, was causing, and seemed to want to confide in her sister.

It was an extra worry that Morag could have done without right then.

'I couldn't believe it when Graham said last week that he wanted to marry me once he was divorced,' Cathy began with a serious note in her voice. 'He'd completely misunderstood me. I was just being sympathetic, but he thought I really cared for him . . . '

'Well, tell him that,' Morag said impatiently. 'Be as blunt — and as firm — as possible.'

'I don't want to be too harsh,' Cathy protested. 'Breaking up with his wife has really hurt him. I don't want to make things any worse.'

'Cathy, the longer you let this go on, the harder it will be,' her sister said firmly. 'Put a stop to it, now.'

Cathy said nothing, going over the situation in her mind once again. When she'd first agreed to let Graham rent the spare bedroom in her flat, he'd seemed to be coping with his problems. But lately he'd become very possessive, and she felt out of her depth.

If she was completely honest with herself, she was afraid. Somehow he seemed to be taking away her freedom, pressing her to make decisions she'd never even considered.

'This is it,' Morag pointed out as they drove up to Olivia's house.

Cathy gazed up at the handsome stone frontage.

'I didn't realise it was so grand.'

'There's always a home for you here, don't forget,' Morag reminded her.

Cathy felt like screaming at being told that again. She desperately wanted to find a way to come here and blot out the last week — but how could she, without telling her parents about Graham?

Jemima opened the door for them.

'Your father and mother have gone back to the hospital. Tom's doing fine — he's regained consciousness and they've set his leg,' she reassured them, all the while looking closely at Cathy.

'Katie Kinloch — you're her double!' she proclaimed triumphantly.

'And so this is Cathy,' Olivia Kinloch said, when they entered her room. 'You're just like my mother!'

Cathy smiled uncertainly at this unexpected greeting. It was disconcerting being compared with relatives she'd never known.

Then Gordon got up from his chair by the fire and saved her from having to reply.

He shook hands with Olivia.

'It's time I was getting back to work,' he said, looking deliberately at Morag., willing her to accompany him.

'I'll see you to the door.'

Morag led the way out, hoping with all her heart that he didn't want to start discussing their relationship again.

With all the upheaval and worries just now she couldn't handle that. But she soon realised that he was still disturbed by the accident.

'It's a relief that Tom has come round. He seemed so badly concussed in the ambulance. And, with a compound fracture — you realise he might not be able to play football again?'

'Oh, no!' Morag was aghast. 'That would break his heart. Tom lives for Kilbarton Athletic.'

Gordon took her hand in his and she moved instinctively towards him . . .

Then Cathy's voice suddenly interrupted them.

'Gordon, would you drop me off at my flat?' she asked him. 'I want to pick up some night clothes. Aunt Olivia has suggested that I should stay here tonight, until we find out how Tom is.'

'No problem.'

Gordon let Morag's hand go as Cathy hurried past the two of them and out of the door to the car.

'Things will work out,' he murmured to Morag, kissing her quickly on the forehead before following Cathy.

Morag was surprised at how unsettled

his abrupt departure with her sister made her feel.

A strange feeling, almost like fear, fluttered in her throat — and the sudden thought that it might be jealousy was even more perturbing.

She immediately dismissed it.

★   ★   ★

In the car, Cathy gave Gordon directions, and soon they drew up outside the tall tenement building in which she lived.

He waited, expecting her to leave, but she sat on.

'Gordon, would you come up to the flat with me?' she asked.

'Well, I really should be getting back to work. Do you need help to carry something?'

'Please! I can't explain it all now. Peggy did say she'd stay in the office till you got back. Please — come up with me!' She caught hold of his arm.

Cathy's urgency puzzled Gordon.

He hadn't had much contact with her over the last few years, as she'd been at teacher training college in Glasgow. Yet here she was now, pleading with him to go into her flat.

'All right — if it's that important to you.'

He got out of the car, then remembered Morag's concern about Cathy.

'Has this got something to do with your flatmate?' he asked.

Cathy was in front of him and she swung round, as if she was going to deny it. Then she met Gordon's direct gaze and nodded.

'I'd appreciate your company,' she said lamely.

They trudged up to the third floor. As Cathy rummaged in her handbag for the keys, the door opened.

'I hope that family of yours appreciate you . . . ' Graham Bateman began, then stopped as the tall figure of Gordon came into view.

'This is Gordon, an old family friend,

Graham. Gordon, meet Graham. I've just come back to pick up a few things. Tom had an accident playing football today and he's in hospital. I'm going back to my aunt's to stay with my family tonight.'

'But what can you do, Cathy?' Graham was dismissive. 'You'd be as well staying here, out of the way.'

'Her mother and father would appreciate her support at this difficult time,' Gordon said firmly, annoyed by Graham's patronising tone.

'Well, have it your way,' Graham said casually. 'After all, I'm just the lodger — isn't that right, Cathy?'

But Cathy fled to her bedroom without answering and began filling a suitcase with everything and anything that came to hand.

'I'll probably be away for a few days,' she explained to Graham when she came out carrying the large case.

It was as if she had to excuse herself, Gordon thought, as he took the case from her.

And this eagerness to get away from her own flat puzzled him . . .

'I take it you'd like a lift back to your aunt's?' he asked.

'Oh, yes, please,' Cathy answered gratefully.

Gordon's face was serious as they drove off.

He'd seen Graham Bateman watching them from the third floor window, and it worried him that the man's possessions were all over the flat. It was as if he owned the place — and Cathy . . .

'He seems to have taken over,' Gordon said.

When Cathy didn't answer, he went on, 'Or does he have your full approval?'

'No!' Cathy's denial was swift. 'I wish I'd never agreed to let him rent the spare bedroom. He's drawing me into his marriage break-up, as if I'm involved somehow.'

'Then why not give up the flat and move into your aunt's?'

Cathy sighed.

'That's what Morag suggested, too. But it's tricky, because Graham Bateman is my immediate boss at work.'

'Then put in for a transfer.'

Cathy shrugged.

It was all very well for other people to give her advice, but Graham Bateman had so much control over her life.

He would be the first to know she wanted a transfer at work, and it was in his power to refuse it.

After a moment, Gordon broke the silence.

'What you need is a night out — something to take your mind off all this. Why don't you go to Lorna's 'cheese and wine' tomorrow night? It's in aid of a good cause — the Red Cross Ball — and there'll be lots of people there that you know.

'It would be far better than spending your evenings with a middle-aged married man,' he added.

For a moment Cathy wanted to giggle — Gordon sounded a bit like a disapproving Victorian father. But then that constant nagging fear returned, as the sensible side of her nature agreed with him — she was out of her depth now, and scared.

★　★　★

It was supper time that Saturday evening before Simon and Helen Kinloch returned from visiting Tom in the hospital.

They both looked exhausted.

'Tom's very tired. The doctor said they'd have a better idea of how he's doing in the morning,' Simon told Morag and Cathy.

Helen looked round their new, lofty-ceilinged lounge. Their own furniture had been placed haphazardly alongside Olivia's pieces.

There were no ornaments, and the room had an uninviting bareness. Her soul silently cried out for her comfortable, modern home, and the happy, uncomplicated life they'd had there.

She was grateful, though, that the two girls had unearthed enough crockery and cutlery to set the table, and that they'd put a casserole in the oven.

'Thanks, both of you. The last thing I wanted now was to prepare a meal,' she said gratefully.

'And it's so good to have you here, too, Cathy,' she added, as her younger daughter brought in the steaming casserole.

Helen rushed to get a place mat for her to set it down, as Morag followed with warm bread and a dish of butter.

They were soon enjoying the meal — everyone except Cathy.

Her mother was quick to notice that she was hardly eating at all.

'Aren't you hungry, Cathy?' she asked.

'No — I had a big lunch,' the girl excused herself.

'But that was nearly eight hours ago,' Helen pointed out.

'Maybe I've just got out of the way of eating good food!' Cathy flashed a brilliant smile, and made a show of eating heartily.

Morag's heart sank. Her mother was not stupid. Cathy was being evasive again, and Helen would want to know the reason this time.

Next morning an unsmiling Michael McQuade, Herald Motors' chief mechanic, arrived at the house.

He seemed wary of Simon Kinloch at first, remembering his unwillingness to accept the job at Herald Motors. But the awkwardness gave way to concern when he heard about Tom.

'Oh, I wouldn't have called round if I'd known,' Michael apologised.

'That's all right. Morag and Cathy are visiting Tom just now — we're going in this afternoon. It would be good to have a look around while the place is quiet,' Simon reassured him.

It was a strange experience for Simon Kinloch, returning to Herald Motors after a gap of twenty-five years.

There had been many changes, yet on the whole it was much as he remembered it.

The buildings and garage forecourt

had been modernised and upgraded, and the showroom had been extended.

Inside, though, the changes were more extensive. The entire complex had been equipped with the very latest technology.

Michael McQuade was proud of the modern equipment.

'The only thing I can't work is the computer.' He gestured round the office. 'Nessie Louden, who was the junior typist here in your day, is in charge of all that.'

Simon smiled. 'Nessie! I remember her! How is she getting on?'

'I don't know what we'd do without her. It was Nessie who first told me about the missing stock.'

'Do you suspect anyone?'

'No. Everyone who works here is completely trustworthy. I just don't know where to start . . . ' Michael broke off, aware of a faint sound outside.

He strode to the door and opened it abruptly.

A stout, white-haired man stood on

the threshold. He looked annoyed at Michael's sudden appearance. Then he saw Simon Kinloch.

'Hello, Simon — I heard you were taking over. It's good to see you again.'

'Andy Davison!' Simon responded warmly, recognising the man as an old acquaintance and long-time customer of Herald Motors.

★ ★ ★

The two men were soon discussing the success of Andy's company, Davison Car Hire, for which Herald Motors held the service contract.

'I take it you know how these things work?' Andy nodded to the computer screens. 'They're a hobby of mine.'

Simon shook his head. 'No, I'm a computer illiterate!'

'It doesn't matter — Nessie's the expert!'

'She must have changed since my day then!' Simon joked.

Time passed swiftly for him as he

caught up on news, but he soon sensed feelings were strained between Michael and Andy.

After Andy had left, Simon and Michael lingered in the office, drinking coffee and chatting about the business.

The conversation soon turned to Andy Davison.

'Does Andy still try to get big discounts on repair prices?' Simon asked. 'He always used to!'

'He still does,' Michael said. 'He's never satisfied with the price I quote. He stands over the mechanics when they're working on his vehicles — and he's always snooping around.

'He's got worse since Miss Kinloch stopped coming in. He already gets a five per cent. discount, but I doubt if he'd be content if we were doing his work free,' Michael finished sourly.

That Sunday evening Morag and Cathy were unusually subdued. Their visit to the hospital had been disturbing — they'd both been upset to see Tom lying in bed, looking so pale and ill.

And they had worked all afternoon, shifting furniture into position and emptying packing cases, while their parents were with Tom.

Morag shook her head.

'I'm glad this weekend's almost over,' she said wearily. 'It's been awful — for everyone.' She sat down heavily.

'I knew I wouldn't feel like going to a cheese and wine party back in Kilbarton tonight,' she said.

'Then phone Lorna and tell her,' Cathy suggested.

'I can't — she's arranged for Max to come to collect me.'

'Are those two back together again, then?'

'Oh, who knows with Lorna? Underneath that bubbly personality, I think she's really quite scared — she doesn't want to be hurt again.'

'I thought I might come along tonight, too — if Max doesn't mind an extra passenger,' Cathy said casually.

'That's a great idea — it'll do you good to have a night out,' Morag said.

The cheese and wine evening was being held in the waiting area of Lorna's father's surgery.

The chairs were pushed back against the walls, and a long trestle table had been placed down one side of the room. It was groaning with glasses, bottles and huge platters of food.

As usual Morag found herself helping Lorna to serve the food and drink.

Many of the people she knew in Kilbarton had heard about Tom's accident, and she spent much of the evening telling them how he was and thanking them for their concern.

She was struck by how at ease Max seemed. He knew very few of the people there, but he was managing to join in conversations.

He certainly had a talent with people, she thought. Not for the first time, she wondered what had really happened between him and Lorna in London.

Halfway through the evening Gordon McEwan arrived, and drew Morag from behind the trestle table, put a glass of white wine in her hand, and guided her over to a quiet corner.

'Let someone else take over for a while,' he said. 'I want to talk to you about Cathy and her flatmate.'

'It's a mess, isn't it?' Morag sighed.

'Cathy's backed herself into a corner, and she seems to think there's no way out.'

'How involved is she? Do you think she is having an affair with him?' Gordon asked bluntly.

'I've never asked her that.'

'Do your parents know what's going on?'

'No. I didn't want to give them anything else to worry about.'

Gordon frowned.

'I don't like that man, Morag. I really do think your parents should be told, despite what Cathy says. Just look at her — I've never seen her so depressed.'

Morag looked across the crowded room to where Cathy was sitting with Jamie, Lorna's younger brother.

Jamie Stewart was a medical student,

and he'd had a crush on Cathy for years. She'd always encouraged him before, but now he was doing all the talking, while Cathy sat beside him in silence.

'Leave it with me. I'll think of something,' Morag said, although she had no idea what she was going to do.

Another Crisis

On the way home in the car, Cathy broke the silence. 'I'm going to the Kilbarton Red Cross Dance next Saturday, too. Jamie Stewart asked me tonight.'

Morag's spirits lifted. 'Great, that makes six of us.'

'I hope so.' Cathy sighed sadly, and Max glanced quickly at her in surprise. And Morag felt a sudden pang of fear for her sister.

This was so unlike Cathy . . .

Max dropped them at their new home, and they hurried up the stone steps to the front door.

Morag put out her hand to stop Cathy going inside.

'Cath, I think you should tell Mum and Dad about Graham. They'll be upset if someone else tells them, you know.'

Cathy pulled away. 'Oh, stop fussing, Morag,' she protested. 'I know what I'm doing. And I don't want you saying anything, either.'

She pushed the door open and hurried up the stairs.

Morag followed slowly, frustrated by Cathy's attitude.

Surely she could see it was wrong to keep their parents in the dark about Graham Bateman, when so many other people knew what was going on?

Ahead of her, Cathy stopped on the stairs.

Jemima was waiting for them on the landing. 'Your Aunt Olivia wants to see you both right away,' she announced. She paused and looked steadily from Cathy to Morag. 'She had a telephone call tonight — from Graham Bateman!'

Jemima led Morag and Cathy to the door of their aunt's room.

'Just go in — your aunt's waiting for you. It's time I was getting to my bed.'

They entered with some foreboding, both bewildered as to why Graham

Bateman should have phoned Aunt Olivia.

Olivia Kinloch was sitting up in bed, with a thick shawl swathed round her shoulders. The bedside lamp cast shadows on her features, softening her face and making her look years younger.

The illusion was shattered as soon as she spoke, for her tone was severe.

'Who is Graham Bateman?' she demanded. 'And why does he feel he has the right to phone me up and argue that I shouldn't encourage you to stay here with your family, Cathy?'

Morag said nothing. This was her sister's problem.

Cathy glanced beseechingly at her for support, but Morag shrugged.

'He's your friend. I've never even met him,' she said quietly.

After an agitated pause, Cathy turned to Olivia, a sudden smile on her face.

'Graham is my flatmate,' she said smoothly. 'I think he was probably just concerned that I'd moved out and left

116

him holding the rent book!'

Aunt Olivia snorted.

'Not a bit of it! He knew Tom was in hospital, but he didn't see why you should stay here when you've a flat of your own. He even tried to talk me into agreeing with him.'

'That's Graham! He's very opinionated.' Cathy tried to laugh it off, but her aunt was not so easily deflected.

'He gave me the impression that he was more than just your flatmate, Cathy. Is he your boyfriend?'

'Oh, no! No!' Cathy's denial was vehement.

'Well, he seems to think he is!' Aunt Olivia told her.

Morag watched closely, feeling almost sorry for her sister.

Olivia Kinloch was one person who would not be fobbed off with a pretty smile and winning ways.

'Well, he's mistaken,' Cathy argued. 'I've never promised him anything.'

'He told me he's going to marry you once he's divorced,' Aunt Olivia paused. 'He spoke to me for about half an hour, and was very serious indeed. He asked me if I thought your parents would be happy for you.'

Cathy sat down heavily and Morag was alarmed to see that tears were trickling down her sister's face.

'I take it they have no idea what's going on.' Aunt Olivia sighed. 'This puts me in a very difficult position, you know.

'Your parents still don't really trust my motives in offering your father a job — and if I become involved in their family problems they may think their suspicions have been confirmed. But if I say nothing, and they then find out I knew all along — well, you can see how that would look.

'Do you have any idea what you're going to do about this man, Cathy?' Olivia Kinloch asked in frustration.

'That's the trouble. I just don't know what to do,' Cathy said, close to tears once more. 'I never intended this to happen. As far as I'm concerned,

Graham's just a friend, nothing more. He's the one who seems to be reading more into it.'

'Cathy, you're the only one who can sort this mess out,' Olivia said gently.

'I know — unless . . . ' Cathy looked towards her sister, her eyes bright with tears. 'Morag, would you help me? You could go to see Graham, and tell him to leave me alone.'

'I wouldn't know where to start,' Morag protested.

'Maybe it wouldn't be such a good idea,' Cathy said quickly, sensing Morag's reluctance. 'I'll just stay here with the family. He'll soon get the message.'

Olivia Kinloch's eyebrows raised as if she doubted matters would work out so neatly.

'I wish I could be so confident.' She shook her head. 'But, Cathy, I do think you should tell your mother. I don't want to be involved in any of this — and you can tell Graham Bateman that, too. There are to be no more latenight phone calls.'

'I feel like running away,' Cathy burst out dramatically. 'I don't even like him any more. I don't want him near me.'

'Then you must tell him that.'

Olivia Kinloch sighed heavily, glancing at the clock as if to indicate that it was time for bed.

★　★　★

A little later Morag crept under her duvet and lay looking round her new room. It seemed so unfinished and impersonal.

Some of the furniture from her old room in the bungalow stood beside Olivia's handsome Edwardian pieces.

Unexpectedly, she felt a wave of loss that she would never see that room again. She felt nostalgic, too, about life in Kilbarton, with its familiar faces and well-known routine.

She rebuked herself almost immediately. She'd wanted a new job, hadn't she — and tomorrow she would start work in the bridal salon.

But then she sighed, for how could she feel happy when Tom was lying in hospital? Or when Cathy was so distraught?

Morag tossed and turned.

She'd work in a garage for the rest of her life without complaint, if only the worries would disappear.

She wished she could talk it all over with Gordon, as she'd once been able to do. But their relationship had changed so much that she no longer knew where she stood with him.

It was bound to happen at some stage, she thought wearily — they wanted such different things from life. Then sleep overtook her . . . It had been a long day.

But Cathy was wide awake.

She sat on the bed in Tom's room, staring at the signed football which had pride of place on the chest of drawers. It was upsetting to think of him lying alone in a hospital bed: He'd looked so ill yesterday, too.

With a sobbing cry, she covered her face with her hands.

She couldn't stop thinking about Graham's phone call to Aunt Olivia. It seemed he would stop at nothing to keep a hold on her. She felt trapped by him, and she knew she had to find a way out.

She stood up distractedly, and her worried features confronted her in the mirror.

'It's all your fault,' she told her reflection severely. 'You didn't exactly discourage him, did you? You were flattered to have an older man flirting with you . . . '

She knew she couldn't involve her parents. They had enough to worry about, with Tom in hospital and her father's new job . . .

Suddenly, she knew what she had to do. The knowledge both terrified and excited her.

While the house and its occupants slept, its windows dark, only the attic room light burned on for several more hours.

Cathy made careful plans for what she was about to do. Nothing could be left to chance.

Next morning, when Morag walked into the small kitchen, her mother was stacking dishes in cupboards.

'Your dad has gone to Herald Motors.' She straightened up, looking at Morag with a smile. 'And Cathy was up and away even before him. When I've finished here, I'm going to visit Tom.'

'It'll be strange for you, not joining us at work some time during the day. And for me, too — the bridal salon is quite a change from the garage,' Morag said thoughtfully.

'Cathy was more like herself this morning,' Helen Kinloch remarked. 'She took that black plastic bag with your old clothes in it. She says she knows someone at work who could use them.'

Morag smiled and busied herself with making a cup of tea.

She was a little surprised that Cathy had taken her old clothes, as she hadn't mentioned them before.

A little later Morag walked the short distance to the salon, her mind full. She was dreading her parents' reaction when they found out about Graham Bateman.

The truth was bound to come out sooner or later, and she knew they would worry about Cathy. They wouldn't approve, either, of the fact that Graham Bateman was a married man.

Tom's accident had devastated them — Cathy's predicament would only add to their problems.

Morag reached the shop and found to her surprise that she was the first to arrive. She opened up with the set of keys her aunt had given her and began to tidy the salon.

Lorraine arrived ten minutes later.

'Oh, I'm sorry I'm late!' she gasped, heading for the back shop. 'I had a row with my boyfriend last night. I didn't get to sleep till all hours.'

Morag went on tidying up as

Lorraine chatted away.

'It's great that you've caught on to what has to be done first thing,' she said. 'The vacuum's been playing up recently, so the carpets haven't been cleaned for a day or two.'

Morag took a look at the vacuum cleaner and found that her mechanical background came in handy.

She emptied the machine, rewired the plug and oiled the moving parts. The vacuum was soon purring over the heavy pile.

Lorraine was grateful. 'I'll finish that off,' she offered, taking the vacuum cleaner from Morag.

'Now, how about doing me another favour?' she asked.

'I know you're good at paperwork, and there's a desk full of it in the office. If you can sort it out you'll be my friend for life!' She took Morag through to the small office which was furnished with a desk and a couple of chairs. Piles of papers and unopened mail were scattered across every surface.

Morag sat down to work and steadily reduced the chaos, until Lorraine interrupted her.

'Morag, I need you — there's a customer!'

A pretty young woman, who was accompanied by her mother, was looking through the rails of wedding gowns.

'Morag will show you what they look like,' Lorraine announced cheerfully.

So, for the next hour, Morag found herself modelling beautiful wedding gowns.

She felt pleased when the customer decided on a dress, and Lorraine measured her up to have the gown specially made.

Morag realised then what her aunt meant about Lorraine being a good saleswoman. She had a real flair for it.

★ ★ ★

After lunch Lorna Stewart paid an unexpected visit to the shop. 'Looking for a wedding dress?' Morag teased.

'No, I'm not! Mind you, you never know! Max wants to stay up here — and he's been hinting about settling down. What do you think of him as husband material?'

'I haven't been measuring him up for the job!' Morag laughed. 'He does seem very charming, though.'

'And he flirts with every girl he meets!' Lorna sighed.

'That's not fair, Lorna. He talks to everyone he meets — male or female. He just seems to be genuinely interested in people.'

'I suppose you're right. But I don't mind when he talks to men, or children, or little old ladies . . . '

'You mean you're jealous!'

'Insanely!' Lorna groaned. 'There, I've admitted it!'

Morag laughed.

'Could we talk somewhere in private?' Lorna asked suddenly. 'It's about Cathy!'

Morag stared at her friend. 'Cathy?'

she repeated in surprise.

Lorna nodded.

The two girls went through to the back shop and were soon sitting in the little office, clutching mugs of tea.

'There are all sorts of stories going about in Kilbarton . . . ' Lorna started hesitantly ' . . . about Cathy and her flatmate, Graham Bateman.'

Morag nodded. She had been expecting this to happen.

'What have you heard?' she asked quietly.

Lorna paused, surprised by Morag's quick response.

'That he's left his wife for her,' Lorna went on after a moment. 'Then he persuaded her to let him move into her spare room. Now it seems he's acting as if he owns her — and, by all accounts, Cathy's scared.

'I was told this by a woman who teaches at the same school. She's very concerned about Cathy, and she thinks this Bateman character is behaving irrationally.'

'That fits in with what I already know.' Morag sighed. 'Cathy's moved into Aunt Olivia's in the hope that'll get rid of him.'

'That sounds like a good idea. I'm sorry to bring you such bad news, Morag, but I thought you should know.'

'I appreciate that,' Morag said with a sigh.

'Oh, try not to worry, Morag,' Lorna said. 'I'm sure Cathy will be fine — you'll see. She and Jamie will have a great time at the dinner dance.'

Lorna left soon after, but Morag couldn't stop thinking about what her friend had said. It made it difficult to concentrate on work, and she was grateful for Lorraine's constant chatter as the afternoon wore on.

At closing time Morag hurried home to tell Cathy about what Lorna Stewart had said.

Cathy smiled dismissively.

'Oh, don't worry about me, Morag! Everything's under control. It's lucky that I'm going away for the rest of the week — I've been asked to help supervise some pupils on a school trip. That should give Graham plenty of time to cool off.' She spoke lightly, as if it was of no importance.

'I wish I could be here for Mum and Dad, though,' she added, her tone more serious. 'The news from the hospital isn't so good. The doctor thinks Tom may need an operation — they're not happy about his progress.'

Morag frowned.

She'd been so occupied with worrying about Cathy today that all thoughts of Tom had been pushed to the back of her mind.

'You and I can still visit Tom tonight, as we planned,' Cathy went on.

She seemed so very normal that, looking at her, Morag wondered if maybe she'd allowed her imagination to run riot.

Perhaps things weren't as bad as she'd feared . . .

As they wandered through to the lounge the phone rang, and their father came out to answer it. He smiled at them both as he saw them there in the hall. But his expression soon darkened as he listened to the voice at the other end of the line.

Morag and Cathy stopped and their mother, sensing that something was wrong, came to the door of the kitchen to listen.

Simon Kinloch put the phone down gently.

'Tom's been rushed into the operating theatre. His condition deteriorated rapidly this afternoon.' His voice shook.

Helen stood in the doorway looking at them in dismay.

'I knew things weren't right today. Tom was very confused, and he seemed to be in pain. We must go to him right away.'

'No!' Simon spoke more sharply than he intended, concerned, now, for his wife. 'He can't have visitors tonight. The Charge Nurse says she'll phone as soon as . . . as there's any news.'

'Come on, Mum — sit down. Morag

and I will see to the meal.' Cathy took charge and gently led Helen to a seat in the lounge.

Simon Kinloch massaged tired eyes.

'It's just one crisis after another, isn't it?' he said wearily. 'When will it ever end?'

★   ★   ★

The four of them sat down to their meal in worried silence. 'Was your first working day with Herald Motors difficult, Simon?' Helen asked at last, trying to behave normally.

'No, I got a great welcome,' he said, carefully keeping his voice level. 'All the men are really keen to make the business profitable again.'

Helen's face brightened at his optimism.

If Simon could settle in easily at Herald Motors, that would be one less thing for her to worry about.

'And the office — has it changed much from my day?'

'Oh, yes. It's all electric typewriters, word processors and computers now. Nessie Louden's in charge — you remember her, don't you?'

'Nessie — of course!' Helen smiled.

'She does most of the work on computer now. Remember all the trouble you had with those work sheets . . . ?' Simon began, and Helen nodded, her interest caught in spite of her worries about Tom.

Cathy and Morag glanced at each other, relieved that their father was distracting their mother for a few moments.

They were clearing the meal away when Gordon McEwan arrived. He'd called into the hospital to visit Tom, but had been told he was still in the operating theatre.

Helen made Gordon a coffee while Simon Kinloch updated him on Tom's condition. After a while, Gordon stood up to leave, realising that the family needed to be alone at this difficult time.

'Gordon, would you mind giving me

a lift back to my flat so I can collect some more things?' Cathy asked suddenly.

Gordon glanced towards Morag but she was avoiding catching his eye.

He shrugged.

'OK. Morag, would you like to come along, too?'

'Oh, good idea,' Cathy murmured without enthusiasm.

'No, I'll wait with Mum and Dad for the news from the hospital,' Morag replied, very aware that Cathy wasn't keen on her accompanying them.

The realisation hurt her.

'Cathy seems so much brighter,' Helen remarked after they'd left. 'I was getting quite worried about her.'

'There's nothing like a crisis to make everyone pull together, is there?' Simon put in.

Morag didn't share their lack of concern.

Why was Cathy going back to the flat?

Gordon watched while Cathy hurried

around the flat, snatching up articles and thrusting them into black plastic bags.

'Has your flatmate left?' he asked.

'No, he's away on a residential course for a few days.'

Gordon noticed how methodically she worked. As she finished with each bag, she attached a prepared label, and placed it beside a pre-packed suitcase in the hall.

'Are you moving in with your parents permanently now?' he asked.

It was a few moments before Cathy answered.

'I've got to get away from this place,' she said urgently.

Gordon stared at her. She hadn't answered his question and she was behaving quite oddly.

'That's it, all done! Let's go,' Cathy announced, seizing an armful of bags.

Gordon picked up the suitcase and the remaining bags, and edged his way out of the door.

Cathy stopped suddenly.

'Just go on, Gordon,' she said. 'I've left something in the fridge.' And she dashed back into the kitchen, closing the door behind her.

She stood leaning against it for a moment, her eyes tightly closed. Then she pulled herself together and, taking an envelope from her pocket, placed it by the kettle.

Graham would see it there when he returned at the end of the week.

Gordon dropped Cathy off at Olivia Kinloch's house and helped her put her bags in her room.

Simon was speaking on the phone, and Morag whispered to them that the charge nurse on Tom's ward had just called.

'It's good news,' Simon announced, replacing the receiver. 'Everything's gone according to plan, and he'll be fit to have visitors tomorrow.'

'Oh, thank goodness!' Helen sighed.

That evening, Cathy was at her most lively, trying to lift everyone's spirits.

★ ★ ★

Morag made an effort to be bright, too, but something niggled. She was sure Cathy was up to something.

Perhaps she'd decided to forget about Graham — but was it possible that she'd set her sights on Gordon, instead.

She dismissed the thought almost immediately. It was so very improbable, yet it left a little ache of sadness round her heart.

'Morag, there's a new Italian restaurant not far from here that's supposed to be very good. How about trying it now for a little supper?' Gordon asked as he was leaving.

The invitation was so unexpected that Morag faltered.

'Tonight! But it's nearly nine o'clock!'

'Yes, why not?' her mother put in. 'It would do you good.'

Half an hour later Morag was sitting opposite Gordon in a candlelit corner of the small restaurant. The waiter had brought menus, but Morag had hardly glanced at hers. 'What's happened to us?' Gordon asked bluntly, watching her.

Morag looked up and met his steady gaze, wondering how to reply. She knew what he meant, but she had no idea how to begin answering him without saying the wrong thing.

'Gordon, so much has happened recently. But, right now, all I can think about is Tom — and as for Cathy . . . ' her voice tailed away.

She bowed her head and looked down at the red and white checks of the tablecloth through a mist of tears.

'I'm sorry, Morag. I seem to have a knack for saying the wrong thing,' Gordon mumbled apologetically.

Morag glanced up, touched that Gordon had realised he'd been tactless.

Her response was gentle. 'It's true — we haven't been on the same wavelength recently,' she said.

'It's my fault! I was so pushy, insisting that we make our relationship more serious,' he said quietly. 'It was completely the wrong time, what with the business being sold, and moving house.'

Gordon seemed anxious to clear up all misunderstandings.

Morag sat back, looking intently at him.

Her spirits lifted a little at the thought that he wanted to return to their old, warm friendship, too — and that he was just as troubled as she was by the rift which had grown between them.

Impulsively, she put her hand out and covered his.

'Let's forget it, and try to get back to the way things were before. Maybe when life settles down — when Cathy's sorted herself out and Tom is well — we'll be able to concentrate on us.'

'That's fine by me.' He grinned and suddenly, despite the smart clothes, he was the old Gordon again.

She knew, at that moment, that she did indeed care deeply for him . . .

Their food arrived just then, and they started to eat.

'Why did Cathy want to go back to the flat?' Morag was still anxious about her sister.

'I think she took everything that belonged to her.' Gordon described the labelled plastic bags.

Then he frowned.

'The strange thing is, two days ago it worried me to see Bateman's things all over the flat.

'But when we went back today, the place had been thoroughly cleared out. Nothing of his was in sight.'

'But when could Cathy have cleared the flat?'

'I don't know. Maybe she didn't go to school today, and did it then.'

Morag put down her knife and fork, and looked at him thoughtfully.

It was the only reasonable explanation.

She told Gordon about Aunt Olivia's phone call from Graham Bateman, and about Lorna's unexpected visit that afternoon.

Morag shook her head.

'What do you think Cathy's up to? She won't tell me anything.'

Gordon was silent for a moment.

'We've all tried to help and advise her,' he pointed out. 'But when it comes down to it, Cathy has to make her own decisions. I think we just have to let her get on with it. Any mistakes she makes will be her own.'

If only it was that simple, Morag thought. But so often she ended up being the one who picked up the pieces from Cathy's mistakes.

I'm Trisha Holden

The next few days seemed never-ending for the Kinlochs, as they waited to hear if Tom's operation had been successful.

Helen spent most of her time by his bed, and Simon and Morag joined her whenever they could. Gordon was a constant visitor, too. They all watched Tom's gradual recovery with grateful relief.

Cathy phoned every day from the school trip she was on, and was overjoyed on Thursday evening at the good news.

Tom was out of danger, they had been told.

'That's fantastic!' Cathy cried. 'I don't think I could have lived with myself if he hadn't been OK.'

It struck Morag that that was a strange thing to say, but she quickly put it down to Cathy's relief.

Morag went into the bridal salon next day with a light heart, happy that Tom was recovering, and delighted that she and Gordon were getting on so well together again after their recent differences.

She was humming happily as she tidied around in the shop when Lorraine arrived, carrying the mail. She carelessly thumbed through the envelopes.

'Here's one for you,' she said.

Morag took it, then froze as she recognised Cathy's handwriting. She tore the envelope open and read the contents.

'Bad news?' Lorraine asked, looking curiously at her.

'Yes! Look, I've got to make a phone call,' Morag said distractedly, hurrying into the office.

She slumped down on the chair and spread the letter on the desk.

Dear Morag, she read. *After Graham phoned Aunt Olivia, I realised that the only way to be rid of him was to leave Glasgow.*

It's the only way he'll ever understand that our friendship is finished, and that I don't want anything more to do with him.

For this reason, I've found a job as an au pair in Majorca — drastic, I know, but I have to put as much distance between us as possible.

I have been in London since Tuesday, and will post this letter in the airport on Thursday evening.

Please don't be angry with me, Morag — this is something I have to do. I'll keep in touch. It's a pity about the dinner dance, though. With love, Cathy.

P.S. Please tell Mum and Dad for me.

★ ★ ★

Cathy's apprehension grew as the plane sped through the darkness. It would be nearly ten o'clock before it touched down at Palma Airport.

She'd been so busy all week that

there had been no time to stop and think about what she was doing.

But now, sitting here on her own, so far from her family and friends, doubts had begun to surface.

She tried to reason them away, telling herself that she was doing the right thing, but the fact remained — she was apprehensive.

'You seem nervous. Is it your first flight?' the white-haired woman next to her asked kindly.

Cathy didn't feel like talking to anyone, but good manners made her reply. 'No, I've flown before, and it doesn't worry me. But this time, I'm on my way to start a new job as an au pair with a family in Majorca.'

The older woman smiled.

'I'm sure you'll enjoy it. Majorca's a lovely island — and I should know! I spend most of the year in my apartment there.'

Cathy smiled politely and turned back to her book.

Her companion took the hint and

remained silent for a while, but when the seatbelt light came on and the plane began to make its descent, she dropped a visiting card into Cathy's lap.

'If you get lonely and feel you'd like to hear another Scottish voice, just give me a call. This is my address.'

'That's very kind of you.' Cathy smiled, telling herself she'd no intention of getting involved with anyone in the next six months — not even this kindly old Scotswoman.

Yet, despite herself, she was intrigued when she saw her travelling companion being met in the arrivals hall by a uniformed chauffeur.

Cathy pushed the trolley with her luggage out into the middle of the hall, looking all around her.

Her new employers had told her she'd be met at the airport, but her name wasn't on any of the cards being held up.

The crowds soon thinned around her as she waited. She could feel herself beginning to panic. What was she supposed to do now?

Someone tapped her lightly on the shoulder and she jumped.

'Excuse me, senorita. Mrs Glencairn asks if you will travel with us.'

Cathy turned and found her travelling companion's chauffeur looking down at her. Before she could answer, he'd taken her trolley from her and started to push it towards the exit.

'No, thank you! My employers are sending someone to meet me,' she protested, but the man continued as if he hadn't heard her.

Outside, she saw her neighbour from the plane beckoning to her from the back of a shining limousine.

'Don't worry — they've probably just mixed up the arrival times.' She smiled. 'If you give me the phone number, Ramon can call them, and say we'll drive you there.'

Cathy silently handed over the scrap of paper on which the address was written. All the confidence of the past week was draining away, and she felt suddenly vulnerable.

'By the way, I'm Isobel Glencairn, but please call me Tibbie.' The elderly woman glanced at the paper and frowned. 'Yes, I thought it would be them. You'd better get in. They go through au pairs at an amazing rate, I'm afraid.'

Cathy swallowed. She hadn't reckoned on her employers being difficult. In fact, she hadn't given them much thought at all. The job had just been the excuse she needed to leave Glasgow — and Graham.

They were soon driving through Palma.

Tibbie pointed out the dramatic 11th-century cathedral, which was floodlit above them, and the many ships and boats whose lights bobbed and twinkled in the bay.

Cathy was polite but distant, determined to keep her new friend at arm's length.

Almost an hour later the car stopped at a heavy wooden gate. Cathy made to get out, but Tibbie put her hand on her arm.

'Don't open the gate — they've got guard dogs. Just ring the bell.'

It was some time before a stout Spanish woman in an apron reluctantly opened the gate.

She spoke rapidly, too fast for Cathy's school Spanish to keep up.

With a loud groan the Spanish woman impatiently beckoned Cathy through the gate. She closed it, shouting at the baying dogs, then walked quickly down the sloping path to a large villa.

Cathy followed, weighed down by her two suitcases. She was furious that the woman was ignoring her, and hadn't even offered to help with her luggage. But she said nothing, following the woman into the house and up flights of tiled steps.

She was gasping for breath when the woman stopped and threw open a door, snapping on a light.

Cathy stared in horror at the chaos in

the room. Torn papers spilled from the bulging waste-paper basket, the bed was a jumble of bedclothes, and the door of the wardrobe hung drunkenly on one hinge.

Face powder and cigarette stubs lay on the dressing-table, and the mirror was smeared with lipstick.

The Spanish woman turned suddenly and saw Cathy's expression of distaste, and for the first time she seemed to soften.

She went out of the room to a cupboard a few doors along and brought out some clean bedlinen, dusters, and a mop and bucket.

She laid the linen on the unmade bed and pointed to the cleaning materials.

The meaning of her gestures was clear. Cathy was expected to clean her own room. It was going to be a long night . . .

★ ★ ★

At almost the same time, in Olivia's room in Glasgow, Simon, Helen and Morag sat round the old woman's bed.

They were still stunned by Cathy's sudden departure — and by the unpleasant visit they'd had that evening from an angry Graham Bateman.

He'd turned up on the doorstep of Olivia's house, demanding to know where Cathy had gone.

His visit had been the first Simon and Helen had heard of his relationship with their daughter.

'It's the secrecy that really gets me!' Simon burst out. 'How could Cathy get herself in a mess like this and not tell us what was going on?'

Helen bit her lip. It was hard to believe that Cathy had been involved with Graham Bateman at all. But he'd told them that Cathy had actually promised to marry him . . .

'I . . . we wanted to tell you, but Cathy said it would only worry you. Tom was so ill at the time, you see . . . ' Morag tried once again to explain the situation, but she knew her parents were deeply upset, and she felt partly to blame.

'It's not your fault, Morag. You're not responsible for Cathy's actions, and you weren't to know what an appalling man Graham Bateman really is,' Olivia Kinloch announced.

She shuddered.

'Poor Cathy! I don't blame her at all for running away. What else could she do?'

Simon and Helen murmured in weary agreement.

'I've had enough for tonight,' Simon said, getting up from his chair. 'I'm going to bed.'

Helen followed him out and, together, they trudged up the stairs to their bedroom.

Helen sank down heavily on to the bed.

'Oh, where did we go wrong, Simon?' she whispered. 'Why did Cathy feel unable to confide in us? Our own daughter doesn't trust us.'

Simon sighed. 'Cathy's a grown woman, love. We have to let her make her own mistakes. We can't expect to be

152

able to protect her for ever.'

'But why didn't she confide in us? We would have helped her. She didn't have to go off to Majorca like that,' Helen protested.

Simon put his arm around her.

'It's Cathy's decision. We have to accept that and get on with our lives.'

He looked down at her and brushed a solitary tear from her cheek.

'It's not as if we'll never see her again, you know,' he reasoned. 'Majorca's not so far away — maybe we could even go out there to visit her! And we can phone her — and write, too.'

'Yes, you're right. We'll keep in touch.'

Helen seemed comforted by his words.

'You know, in the end this might do Cathy a lot of good,' Simon Kinloch went on. 'Perhaps it's time she learned to take more responsibility for her actions. She's always been too quick to let other people sort out her problems for her.'

'I know,' Helen conceded. 'It's just that everyone seemed to know what was going on except us. Morag knew I was worried about Cathy, but she said nothing.'

'We can't blame Morag for that, Helen, after all Cathy asked her not to break her confidence,' Simon pointed out. 'But it's Morag who's been left to explain everything to us as usual.'

'Yes, you're right!' Helen sighed. 'We've always expected so much from Morag. Maybe we've been unfair to her, asking her to work in the garage instead of going to university. 'Oh, I wish . . . '

Simon kissed her softly on the lips to silence her.

'We can't change the past, love,' he whispered, holding her close, his cheek on the silky dark hair that framed her face.

'We just have to get on with our lives now — brooding won't change anything. Let's try to concentrate on the good things that are happening — like

Tom coming home.'

'Yes . . . yes!' Helen nodded. 'That's something to look forward to.'

*   *   *

The following Monday morning Simon Kinloch drove on to the forecourt at Herald Motors.

He frowned when he saw the chief mechanic, Michael McQuade, standing outside the office with Andy Davison.

It was obvious the two men had been arguing, and Simon was annoyed.

Andy was a good customer. He bought the cars for his rental business from Herald Motors, and they couldn't afford to fall out with him.

'I'm just checking up on the progress of those two cars I brought in to be serviced,' Andy greeted him cheerily.

'They only came in yesterday, and at the last minute at that.' Michael McQuade grunted and disappeared into the repair shop.

'Poor old Michael — he really lets

things get to him!' Andy laughed loudly, then turned to Simon.

'What's this about your younger girl packing her bags and running off to Spain?' he asked.

So it was common knowledge already. For the first time, Simon understood Michael McQuade's dislike of this man.

He shrugged carelessly, determined not to let his anger show.

'You seem to know all about it already,' he said casually.

'Oh, I just heard a bit of gossip last night. I wasn't sure whether to believe it or not — especially the part about Cathy being mixed up with a married man.'

Simon ignored the taunt.

'Cathy's always fancied working abroad, so when this job came up she jumped at the chance. It was a good opportunity for her to get away from this Bateman character, too,' he explained.

Andy seemed almost disappointed by Simon's matter-of-fact reply. He had no idea of the effort it had cost.

After a few more minutes discussing the repairs to his two cars, Andy Davison left.

Michael McQuade, watching his departure from the service bay, rejoined Simon at once.

'I suppose you've heard about Cathy, too,' Simon said wearily.

'I hadn't — until Andy Davison took great delight in telling me all about it this morning,' Michael said grimly.

'Well, it's true — Cathy's taken a job as an au pair, in Majorca. She wanted to get away from this Graham Bateman — he just wouldn't leave her alone.'

Michael looked directly at Simon. 'It's none of my business — or anyone else's except Cathy's. No-one will hear of it from me.'

'Thanks, Michael.' Simon smiled.

'Mr Kinloch, could I have a word with you, please?' Nessie Louden, the secretary, called from the open office door. 'It's important.'

'What's wrong, Nessie?' Simon asked, noting how agitated she seemed.

'It's the stock figures again — my computer accounts don't match up. You see, when the stock losses were first noticed, I opened a back-up system. I didn't tell anyone else about it.'

'What have you found?'

Nessie launched into a long description of the two systems.

On the office record, the losses didn't show, but after double-checking with her back-up system she'd found several differences.

'So you're saying that stock has disappeared again? Have you checked with the stores?' Simon asked.

'No. I thought I should tell you first. I've made a list of what seems to be missing.'

Simon Kinloch took the sheet of paper from her.

'It's not as much as before, but the fact that this is still happening is worrying. I'd better tell Michael.'

'Mr Kinloch, do you mind if I make a suggestion?' Nessie asked nervously.

'I could do with some help in the

office — running two systems is so time-consuming — but it would have to be someone we can trust. Do you think Mrs Kinloch would agree to do a few hours in the office?'

Simon smiled, pleased by this suggestion.

He knew that Helen needed something to take her mind off Cathy's problems and, with Tom recovering well, she would soon have lots of spare time. Helen had enjoyed working in the office at Herald Motors before they were married, and he was sure she'd be happy to return.

'That's a good idea. I'll certainly ask her,' he told Nessie.

Simon found Michael in the repair shop, talking to Bertie, who was in charge of the storeroom.

'I had a look around the storeroom this morning and I'm sure some items are missing,' Bertie explained.

Simon showed him Nessie's list, and Bertie confirmed that it tallied with the missing stock.

'We need new locks for the store,' Bertie insisted. 'Somebody's got a key, and they're getting in when we're closed. It's the only explanation.'

'I agree.' Michael nodded.

'Right, I'll have new locks fitted, and only the three of us will have keys,' Simon decided. 'They're not to be lent to anyone.'

'It might be a good idea to do the same for Nessie's office,' Michael suggested.

Simon looked at him. 'Why? There's been no break-in attempted there.'

'We can't be too careful, Simon. There may not be any stock in the office, but there are cheque books, invoices . . . '

'You're right.' Simon nodded, sensing that Michael had other reasons, too.

★　★　★

By the beginning of the next week preparations were underway for Tom's homecoming.

He was desperate to leave hospital, and the doctors had decided that Wednesday would be his big day.

Morag was his only visitor on the Tuesday evening.

Tom was full of excitement, delighted to find that his strength was gradually returning.

'Guess what!' he said as soon as he saw his sister. 'The doctor told me there's no reason why I shouldn't play football again. The break is healing more quickly than expected.

'And — ' he patted his cropped head, where now only a dressing covered the wound ' — I get the stitches out tomorrow! The plaster on my leg will need to stay for a few more weeks, though.'

Morag smiled as he rushed on to talk about his plans for the future.

'Where's Gordon tonight?' he asked suddenly.

'I . . . I don't know — probably working late,' Morag said.

'Have you two had a row?' Tom asked bluntly.

Tact never was his strong point, Morag reminded herself.

'No . . . no . . . not exactly.'

Tom looked critically at his sister.

'Did something happen at the Red Cross Dance in Kilbarton on Saturday night? Gordon came to visit me on Sunday and he never mentioned it once, which I thought was a bit strange.'

Morag would rather not have answered, but Tom was obviously waiting for her reply.

'We didn't have a row or anything,' she began awkwardly. 'It was just — well, I was worried to death about Cathy and I couldn't really think of anything else.'

'I know what you mean — Mum and Dad went on about Cathy for the whole of Saturday visiting hour.' Tom grinned and shrugged. 'They were really upset, so I couldn't say to them it was just like Cathy to skip off to Spain to avoid an awkward situation. You know how she loves a bit of drama!'

Tom's cheerfulness was infectious and Morag had to smile, relaxing at last.

'Now, out with it! What happened on Saturday night?' he asked again, a smile still on his lips.

'It sounds really stupid now, but at the time I was quite hurt by Lorna and Gordon's attitude. I was so worried about Cathy, but they just seemed bored by the whole business.'

Morag told Tom how, halfway through the evening, Lorna had said sharply, 'For heaven's sake, Morag, can we change the subject? I'm fed up hearing Cathy's name.'

To Morag's surprise Gordon had immediately backed Lorna up.

'I second that!' he'd muttered.

'I admire your loyalty,' Lorna had continued dryly. 'But if my sister had left me to explain away the mess she'd created, I don't think I'd be so charitable.

'Cathy will survive, you'll see — and the experience might even do her good,' was Lorna's rather blunt verdict, and Morag had been taken aback by her words.

She'd expected some support.

Morag had been upset about Cathy's sudden departure, but neither Lorna nor Gordon had been sympathetic.

She'd felt especially hurt that Gordon, of all people, should have been so unfeeling . . .

Morag looked ruefully at Tom.

'I suppose I let my hurt and annoyance show.' She sighed. 'The rest of the evening was very awkward, and when it was time to leave I made a point of avoiding both Gordon and Lorna.'

Tom thought about what she'd said for a few moments.

'You know, they didn't mean to upset you, Morag,' he said. 'But maybe, like me, they're tired of seeing Cathy take advantage of you.

'No matter what she does, she lets you pick up the pieces. Maybe she wouldn't have been so quick to run off to Spain if she hadn't had you to explain to Mum and Dad.'

Morag admitted to herself that there was a lot of truth in what her brother had said. Cathy had taken advantage of her . . .

'But that's enough of Cathy!' Tom decided. 'Tell me all about our new home. I've got some catching up to do!'

Morag realised that, underneath the banter, Tom was nervous about seeing their new home for the first time.

He hadn't wanted to move to Glasgow from Kilbarton, but now it had been thrust upon him.

'It's much better than I ever imagined it would be,' she reassured him.

Tom sank back against his pillows in relief, and Morag realised how tired he was. Not long after she stood up with a smile.

Tom grabbed her hand as she was about to leave.

'Thanks — I feel a lot better about the new place now. You're the only one I could ask.'

His words stayed with her, and she felt a little ashamed.

She'd been so immersed in worrying about Cathy that she hadn't realised how Tom was feeling.

★　★　★

Helen and Simon collected Tom from the hospital next morning, and the three of them drove straight back to Aunt Olivia's house.

When the car drew up at his new home, Tom whistled, impressed by the ornate Edwardian façade.

Then he groaned inwardly when he saw the flight of steps which led up to the front door.

'I'm not very good on the crutches yet, Dad,' he said.

'Don't worry — we arranged for Gordon to be here to meet us. We'll get you into the house between us!' Simon smiled.

Just then the front door opened and Gordon came down the steps towards them. It took little effort for the two men to help Tom into the house.

They took him into Olivia Kinloch's room to introduce him to his aunt for the first time.

She shook her head sadly when she saw how pale and gaunt Tom looked.

'At the moment, you're the image of my father — when he was an old man!' she told him.

'It's probably the bald head that does it!' Tom answered cheerfully.

Olivia laughed. She looked at him keenly.

'You're right — that's exactly what it is!'

It was soon evident that the home-coming had exhausted Tom, and Helen suggested he should rest for a while. Simon and Gordon were about to help him up to his room when Jemima suddenly intervened.

'Don't put the boy away up in the attic on his own — he'll be so lonely he'll have a relapse. He could always sleep in the maid's room behind the kitchen for a week or two. That way, he'll be able to get about on his own, and he'll have company.'

Helen and Simon glanced anxiously at one another, concerned that Olivia Kinloch was again attempting to interfere in their lives.

Tom, however, was oblivious to their anxiety.

'That's a great idea!' he said eagerly.

He took up his crutches and swung himself awkwardly after the old woman as she led the way through the kitchen.

The bed in the little back room had already been made up.

Tom collapsed on to the bed, panting.

'Jemima, you and I are going to get along fine!'

'It seemed daft, you being stuck upstairs on your own. And, when you feel strong enough, you can go through to talk with your Aunt Olivia. She'd like that.'

Helen, watching, knew it was a sensible arrangement. Yet she couldn't help worrying that Olivia and Jemima were trying to take her son away from her — for that room had been deliberately prepared for him.

Over the next few days the household settled down.

Tom was delighted with his room on the ground floor, as he was able to hobble to Aunt Olivia's room on his crutches.

He would sit there for hours, fascinated by the stories she told him of the vintage cars the family used to own.

By the following Saturday morning Morag had calmed down about the dinner dance, and realised that she had over-reacted.

She arrived early at the shop, determined to phone Lorna and Gordon to make her peace with them.

As she hung her coat in the office, she heard the door of the salon open. Thinking it would be Lorraine, she did nothing, but when there was no shouted greeting she went out into the main shop.

A young woman was standing by the counter. 'You must be Morag,' she said, holding out her hand. 'I'm Trisha Holden — Cathy and I were at teacher-training college together.

'I helped her to get the au pair job in Majorca — I worked there for six months myself, and I knew that the family were looking for another young girl. Cathy asked me to bring you these.' She held out a bunch of keys. 'They're for her flat in Glasgow. She asked if you'd return them to the landlord for her.'

Morag sighed.

It was typical of Cathy to ask other people to sort out her problems for her.

'Of course,' she said wearily, taking the keys from Trisha. 'It was good of you to bring them.'

'Oh, it was no trouble,' Trisha told her. 'I was passing, anyway. And I was only too pleased to help Cathy out — I know what it's like to be looking for a job.

'But I've been really lucky,' she went

on. 'I've been offered a teaching position in Glasgow. Mr Bateman, the head of the department, phoned this week . . . '

'Graham Bateman?' Morag demanded, panic rising up in her.

'Yes, do you know him? He seems such a nice man — he was really interested in my Spanish teaching experience.'

'Did . . . did Cathy explain to you why she was so anxious to leave Glasgow?' Morag faltered.

'Yes, she did,' Trisha replied. 'But . . . oh, no! Oh, Morag! Don't tell me he's . . . '

Morag sighed.

'Yes, Graham Bateman is the one who made Cathy so miserable.'

It was clear to her why Trisha had been given the job. Now Graham Bateman knew exactly where to find Cathy.

. . . He Wants Proof

Cathy stood on the little terrace outside her bedroom in the warm dusk. She had a fine view of the sea and the pine-covered slopes on the other side of the natural inlet, where lights were starting to twinkle.

An ocean-going yacht, almost as big as a small passenger liner, was anchored out in the middle of the bay.

As she watched, several people who were dressed for dinner climbed down into a powerboat and set off across the water to the yacht club.

Cathy had sometimes dreamed of, one day, being in just such an idyllic location. But in reality, after only a month here, she found no pleasure in the view.

She was homesick and lonely, and she didn't enjoy being treated as one of the servants.

She forced back the tears that threatened to overcome her.

Next weekend was her parents' silver wedding anniversary and she would miss the celebrations that Aunt Olivia was secretly planning. She wouldn't see Tom take his first steps without the plaster cast, either.

The harsh ring of the telephone broke into her thoughts, and she went indoors to answer it.

It was Senora Ramis, her employer.

'Senora Glencairn, my old friend and your countrywoman, has come to visit. She would like to see you. Pilar will bring her up.'

Before Cathy could object the phone was put down.

She glanced round the room, quickly checking that it was presentable.

After living here for over a month it was clean and tidy, with her family photographs and personal possessions giving it a more homely feel.

She looked up to see Tibbie Glencairn standing in the doorway.

'How are you, my dear? I thought, after a month here, that you might welcome a visit from a fellow Scot.'

'Won't you sit down?' Cathy gestured to one of the two small armchairs.

She was lonely, but she didn't want to get involved with anyone — the fewer people who knew who she was, the better. Perhaps she was being over-cautious, but she was scared.

If Graham knew where to find her, there was no telling what he might do.

'I'm glad you're reasonably comfort-able here.' Tibbie glanced approvingly round the room.

'How are the Ramis family to work for? They haven't got a very good record, I'm afraid.'

'I can't complain. Carlos and Maria have been relatively well-behaved so far,' Cathy said, referring to her six-and-seven-year-old charges.

'Do you get much free time?' Tibbie asked. 'What do you do then?'

So many questions!

Cathy felt slightly irritated by Tibbie's curiosity.

'From Monday to Friday, I'm on duty till the children go to bed. Saturday and Sunday are my days off, so I can do as I please then.'

'That seems reasonable. Are they treating you well?'

Cathy bit back her annoyance at being questioned, realising that Tibbie was just trying to be friendly.

'On the whole, yes. But it's not knowing where I fit in that's the problem — I'm not a servant, and I'm not family.'

'You should try to be firm with the servants,' the older woman advised. 'They'll take advantage of you, if you let them. You'll find yourself doing their work.'

Cathy smiled politely.

She'd found that out on her very first evening.

Then her heart sank as Tibbie Glencairn noticed the photographs displayed on her dressing-table.

'Is that your family?' she asked, getting up to have a closer look at a photograph, which had been taken on a family day out the year before.

'Why, that's Largs!' she exclaimed. Then she turned to an old picture of Cathy's father as a young man.

Simon Kinloch was sitting at the wheel of a vintage car, outside his father's business.

'That's Herald Motors! A girl in my class at school used to live there.'

Then Tibbie stopped, and turned to Cathy.

'A family called Kinloch used to own Herald Motors — they probably still do. Are you related?'

Cathy stared numbly at her. She'd come to Majorca to make a fresh start, and in just a few moments she'd met someone who knew her family. She felt suddenly very tired.

'Yes, I am. My grandfather founded the business, and my aunt is the present owner. My father is her manager.'

'That makes sense! Senora Ramis

told me your father managed a garage in Glasgow.'

Cathy paused, wary of Tibbie's interest.

'We only met on the plane a month ago,' she pointed out. 'Why are you so interested in me?'

'Senora Ramis phoned me,' Tibbie explained gently. 'She was puzzled because you've shown no interest at all in going out since you arrived. Usually her trouble is the opposite — au pairs staying out till all hours and not being fit for work the next day.' She looked at Cathy kindly. 'I suggested that perhaps you were lonely and in need of a friend.'

Cathy sighed, deciding to confide in this woman.

'Yes, I am lonely — but that's not why I stay in. I came here to get away from someone — a man. I just don't want to do anything that might enable him to find me.'

'I see.' Tibbie Glencairn nodded. 'In any case, I think you should get out of this room and take some fresh air. It'll make you feel a lot better.'

'I might just do that,' Cathy murmured.

'I'm not taking 'no' for an answer. Why don't we have a swim now, in the pool here?' the other woman suggested. 'My apartment's in the complex next door and we share the pool with these villas.'

'I really don't feel like swimming,' Cathy protested.

'Why not?'

Cathy sighed.

'Because I know that the man I came here to escape has found out where I am. The pool in the complex is visible from the road, and I can't take the risk that he might see me.'

'Surely he wouldn't come this far to look for you?' Tibbie asked.

'You don't know him! I haven't even given this address to my family, in case he managed to get hold of it. But somehow he's tracked down the friend who recommended me for this job.'

Cathy told Tibbie about the letter Morag had sent, warning that Graham Bateman had spoken to Trisha Holden.

'He's probably here by now,' she went on glumly. 'My sister said he'd boasted about having tickets to come out here. He thinks I'll be unable to resist such a romantic gesture.'

Tibbie saw her shudder, and felt Cathy's dread and fear.

'Why don't you come and stay with me in my flat until Monday?' she offered impulsively. 'That way, even if he does turn up, you won't be here.'

Cathy's first reaction was to refuse, but then she wavered.

She was so tired of her own company — and she liked Tibbie Glencairn.

'Yes! Why not! I'll get a few things together. And I'll change out of these old clothes.' Cathy smiled.

'Trisha said I should try to look as plain as possible. According to her, Senora Ramis thinks that she has to protect her young brother, Phillipe, from glamorous au pairs!'

'It hasn't worked.' Tibbie smiled. 'He's noticed you already. He stopped me on my way up here and asked me to introduce you!'

Cathy brightened a little at that.

Phillipe was so handsome! Suddenly her spirits started to rise.

She felt safe with Tibbie — and it was bliss not to be alone any more.

★   ★   ★

I'll put back on all the weight I've lost if I eat this!' Morag put down the huge chocolate egg that Aunt Olivia had given her this Easter morning.

'It's a bit over the top, if you ask me.' Her mother set down an equally-ornate Easter egg beside it. 'I suppose she's just trying to be pleasant, though.'

Morag didn't answer.

She knew her mother still found it difficult to trust Olivia Kinloch.

Surprisingly, her father, who'd been very reluctant to move here, had struck up a good working relationship with his sister.

But Morag still wished that Olivia hadn't decided to surprise Simon and Helen with a party to celebrate their silver wedding anniversary.

It was a well-intended gesture, but Morag was unsure of how her mother would react.

'Mum, there's something you should know,' Morag began uneasily, determined at last to tell her mother the latest news about Cathy.

She'd held it back, not wanting to worry Helen, but her mother had a right to know.

'I think that Graham Bateman has gone to Majorca to try to find Cathy.'

Morag poured out the whole story of how Graham had tricked Trisha Holden into telling him where Cathy was staying.

She'd since heard from Trisha that Graham had booked tickets to fly to Majorca during the Easter holidays.

'Cathy knows — I've written to tell

her,' Morag finished.

Helen sighed.

'Now I can understand why Cathy was so desperate to get away. He just won't give up, will he?'

'Dad should really be told,' Morag murmured.

'I'll tell him later.' Helen frowned. 'He's got enough to worry about at the moment, with stock still going missing from Herald Motors.'

'But I thought the new locks had put a stop to that?'

'So did your father. But when Bert carried out his stock check of the store this morning, he noticed that a box of electrical parts had gone.' Helen sighed wearily.

'I think some of the staff have their suspicions, though,' she added.

'What makes you say that?' Morag asked.

'Well, once or twice when we've been in the office, Nessie has hinted that she has an idea she knows who the culprit could be. She refuses to be drawn, though,' Helen said.

'What about Michael McQuade? Maybe he would tell you more,' Morag suggested, looking at her mother enquiringly.

'I think he has a theory, too, but he says he wants proof before he accuses anyone. Oh, Morag, I don't know what your dad's going to do about it all.'

'So what are you two gossiping about?' Tom asked cheerily, pushing open the door with one crutch.

'We were just talking about Cathy,' Morag told him quickly.

There was no point involving Tom in Herald Motors' problems.

'Not again!' Tom groaned, pulling a face.

'What are you doing up here?' Helen Kinloch asked curiously. 'I thought you were talking to your aunt.'

'I was — but Gordon's just arrived. He and Aunt Olivia are talking business, so I made myself scarce.'

Tom sat down heavily, propping his crutches at the side of his chair.

'Gordon didn't mention anything to me,' Morag said, puzzled.

'It's something to do with vintage cars, I think,' Tom explained. 'Gordon wants to expand his fleet, so that he can do more weddings, and Aunt Olivia has lots of useful contacts.' It was the first Morag had heard of Gordon's plans for expansion, and she felt a little put out.

They'd been getting on so well together lately — yet he still hadn't thought to confide in her.

'I hope you don't mind, Mum — I asked Gordon if he'd like to come up for lunch after he's finished,' Tom went on. 'You're always saying that one more won't make any difference!'

'No, that's fine, Tom.' Helen Kinloch smiled. 'Gordon knows he's always welcome here.'

'Oh, I almost forgot to tell you!' Tom remembered suddenly, and his mother smiled at his excitement. 'I was in one of the lock-ups yesterday, and I saw an old Model-T Ford. I asked Aunt Olivia about it, and she said that if I can get it running then it's mine!'

'Oh, that was your dad's car!' Helen Kinloch said nostalgically. 'At least, he used to drive it, years ago. He used to take me out in it before we were married. He was so proud of it.'

* * *

Simon Kinloch came in just before lunch. Though it was a Sunday, he'd been at Herald Motors all morning.

Helen could tell from his expression that something was wrong.

'Michael was wakened up last night by his dog barking. When he went outside to have a look around he found someone had been trying to force open the lock on the storeroom door. They just won't give up.'

'That's because they're making too much money out of us. Nessie has calculated that we've lost thousands of pounds' worth of stock in the past year,' Helen remarked.

'I know. No business can sustain that

kind of loss indefinitely.' Simon looked grim.

There was a knock at the door and Gordon McEwan came in.

Simon seemed relieved to see him.

'Could you spare me a few minutes? I've got something to discuss with you,' Gordon said.

'Of course. We can talk in here,' Simon replied, pushing open the door of the study.

Again, Morag felt slightly annoyed with Gordon. He usually shared his plans with her — so why was he being so secretive?

Half an hour later Helen looked at her watch. 'Morag, go and tell your father and Gordon that I'm putting lunch on the table,' she said. 'We can't wait all day.'

Morag knocked on the study door and went in without waiting for an answer. Her father and Gordon immediately stopped speaking, and she felt uncomfortable.

It was almost as if they had been

discussing her behind her back.

'Your aunt has made me a very attractive business offer,' Gordon told her, looking very pleased with himself.

'And I've told him he'd be a fool not to accept it,' Simon said.

'I hope it all works out for you, Gordon.' Morag was genuinely pleased for him. She waited for him to tell her more. When he said nothing, she again felt that little stab of hurt and disappointment.

The five of them sat down to lunch, and Tom was soon telling his father about the old Model-T Ford.

Simon Kinloch was amazed.

'Good grief! Is it still around? I can remember taking your mother out in it, on our very first date.'

Helen nodded fondly as he reminisced about the runs they'd had in the car. It was so good to remember the old times.

Tom, as always, was eager to make a start and could hardly wait to drag his father outside to examine the car.

'Hopefully I'll be able to start work on it in a couple of weeks, once I get my plaster off. The doctor said I'd need to get plenty of exercise!'

'He didn't mean working on a car!' His mother laughed.

Tom, with all his enthusiasm, was a joy to have around.

As Simon and Gordon discussed the problems of the motor trade, Helen noticed that Morag was very quiet.

Her head was bent low over her plate, as if she was excluded from the conversation.

It saddened Helen, for she'd always hoped that Morag and Gordon would end up together. But Cathy's problems had affected Morag deeply. She'd always been so easy-going, but lately she seemed tense.

'Great meal, Mum!' Tom declared, helping himself to seconds.

'I'm glad you liked it — I'm tired out making it,' Helen replied.

'I'll clear up, Mum,' Morag offered.

'And I'll help,' Gordon added.

Helen smiled. She'd hoped that Morag and Gordon would offer to help. It would give them a chance to talk. But Tom spoiled her plan almost immediately by announcing that he would help, too.

As the three of them disappeared into the small kitchen, Helen Kinloch knew there would be little serious talking done with Tom there.

But Morag was glad of Tom's company. She wasn't sure what to say to Gordon these days — he seemed to have changed so much.

★   ★   ★

Tom immediately started asking Gordon about his business in Kilbarton.

As Gordon talked about changes he was making, Morag busied herself with drying the dishes.

'I'd really like to come out to Kilbarton and see what you've been doing,' Tom said. 'I'm sure Morag would drive me out tomorrow night.'

189

'Maybe Morag has other plans,' Gordon countered.

'She won't have!' Tom declared. 'You're not doing anything tomorrow night, are you, Morag?'

'No, Tom. And yes, I'll drive you to Kilbarton.'

'Great! I'll see you then, Gordon.' Tom finished the plate he was drying and limped out.

'I hope you don't mind Tom inviting himself over,' Morag said stiffly.

'The Kinlochs are always welcome at my place,' Gordon replied.

There was a long silence between them.

'Morag, I wasn't going to worry you with this, but I think you should know,' he told her. 'I was at the airport last night with a customer, and I saw Graham Bateman checking in for a flight to Majorca.'

Morag smiled wryly.

'It's OK, Gordon. I already know.'

'Then why didn't you tell me?' Gordon demanded.

She stared at him.

'How could I? You told me that you were tired of hearing about Cathy.'

'But this is different!'

'How was I supposed to know that? I've hardly seen you since the Red Cross Dance. Then, when you have been here, you've talked to everyone except me. My whole family knew you were working with Aunt Olivia before I did.'

'That's not true, Morag. You know I — '

'Morag, phone call for you,' her father called, interrupting whatever Gordon had been about to say. 'It's Lorna.'

'Sorry, Gordon — I've got to go,' Morag excused herself, hurrying out of the room.

'Morag, I've something to tell you,' Lorna Stewart said excitedly. 'Max and I are engaged! How do you feel about being a bridesmaid?'

It took a moment for the news to sink in.

'Oh, Lorna, I . . . I couldn't be more pleased,' Morag gasped. 'And of course I'd be delighted to be your bridesmaid.'

'Thanks for not saying, 'It's so sudden,' even if you're thinking it. But Max gave me an ultimatum. He said if I didn't marry him he'd go back to London for ever. So what choice did I have?'

'It sounds very romantic.'

'Yes, I suppose it is! But you do think I've done the right thing, don't you?' Lorna asked suddenly.

'Of course — Max is one of the nicest and kindest men I've ever met,' Morag said truthfully.

'Yes, he is, isn't he? I think that's what bothered me before — I couldn't believe that anyone could be so nice!'

'Your parents must be thrilled.'

'I haven't told them yet — it's only just happened. I wanted you to be the first to know, you see.' A voice sounded in the background. 'Anyway, I'd better go now — we're on our way to break the news to Mum and Dad,' Lorna said hurriedly and Morag had to smile.

'We'll see you on Saturday evening at your parents' party and I'll show you my ring,' Lorna finished and hung up.

Morag was smiling when she replaced the receiver.

Lorna's happiness was infectious.

She ran downstairs to tell everyone the good news, her annoyance with Gordon forgotten.

★   ★   ★

Tibbie Glencairn's apartment was in the middle of an exclusive block in the same complex as Cathy's employer's villa.

The flats were built into the rock face, and entry was by a lift which went downwards from the reception area.

After just a few hours there Cathy felt the tensions easing out of her. Staying in Tibbie's apartment was a world away from her flat in Glasgow.

The marble-tiled floor of the lounge was scattered with fine blue and white rugs. A glass display unit down one wall sparkled with porcelain figures and brightly-painted pottery. Prints of Monet's summer flowers, shimmering in the sunshine, decorated the walls.

For the first time since she left Glasgow, Cathy was able to relax, all thoughts of Graham Bateman forgotten.

Cathy soon found that Tibbie was extremely good company.

She had endless stories to tell of the years she'd spent travelling round the world with her diplomat husband before she was widowed.

On the Saturday afternoon Cathy and Tibbie were relaxing on the shady terrace that overlooked the pool when the front doorbell buzzed.

'I'll get it.' Tibbie got up from her chair and disappeared into the hall.

A few seconds later, Cathy heard Tibbie's voice welcoming their guest.

'Phillipe — what a surprise! Come in, please.'

Senora Ramis' younger brother had

recently been showing more and more interest in Cathy, despite her best efforts to dissuade him.

'We're out on the terrace,' Tibbie said, leading the way through the lounge and out of the patio doors.

'Cathy,' she announced, 'you've got a visitor!'

'Hello, Phillipe,' Cathy said. 'What are you doing here?'

'I have come to see if you would like to have a swim with me,' he said, in his careful English. 'The sun is shining, and it is your day off — what more could we ask for?'

'The sun's too strong in the afternoon,' Cathy protested.

'It's not so bad! Please, Cathy — just for an hour,' he coaxed.

Tibbie, standing behind him, shrugged. She and Cathy had already agreed that Phillipe was too used to getting his own way.

He was a charming young man, but he was also very persistent.

'I'll come down to the pool this

evening,' Cathy told him. 'I'll see you then.'

'It's a date.' He smiled at her, his eyes sparkling.

Not so long ago, Cathy thought, a smile like that would have bowled her over. She'd have been flattered that someone as handsome as Phillipe was so obviously interested in her. But she was wary now, after Graham, with his well-practised compliments and charming smile.

'So that's it settled.' Tibbie looked at her watch. 'Cathy and I will both be at the pool around seven. We'll see you then.'

She smiled graciously at Phillipe, then stood pointedly aside to indicate that he should go.

Tibbie was still smiling when she came back on to the terrace after seeing Phillipe out.

'It looks like you've got yourself an admirer, Cathy!' she teased. 'Phillipe seems very taken with you.'

'He just won't take the hint, will he?'

Cathy groaned. 'He thinks he just has to bat those Spanish eyes of his and I'll fall at his feet!'

She lay back on her sun-lounger and took up her book, but her eyes wouldn't focus on the words.

She'd arranged to meet Phillipe that evening in a glamorous, luxurious setting — but, oh, how she wished it was Jamie Stewart she had a date with, in one of the cosy, familiar pubs of Kilbarton . . .

Later that Saturday evening the pool was pleasantly warm, and very quiet.

Cathy and Tibbie had just finished their swim when Phillipe arrived.

'What's wrong, Phillipe? You don't look very happy,' Tibbie asked, noting his cross expression.

'Cathy didn't tell us that she has a fiancé! He is with my sister just now, very anxious about her. He says he has come to take her back home,' he told them.

Cathy felt the blood drain from her face. She reached behind her for something to hold on to, her head spinning.

'Phillipe, help Cathy — quickly!' Tibbie ordered.

Phillipe moved towards her, his expression concerned, but Cathy waved him away.

She lowered herself on to a sun-lounger and buried her face in her hands. Her shoulders shook as she sobbed quietly.

It had all been for nothing. All the plans, all the sacrifices she'd made — and still Graham Bateman had found her.

Simon's Suggestion

Cathy stood in the lounge of Senora Ramis' villa, staring coldly at Graham Bateman.

Her face grew scarlet with anger, frustration and embarrassment, as she listened to what he had to say.

'You only had to tell me if you wanted to break your promise! You didn't need to run away! As I said to Senora Ramis, everyone at home has been so worried about you. I've come to take you back to Glasgow.'

Cathy took a step towards him, shaking with barely-suppressed anger.

'I never promised you anything, Graham,' she said icily. 'You were the one who decided upon marriage, not me.'

'Now, Cathy, I wouldn't have come all this way if that was the case.' He looked appealingly at Senora Ramis

199

who was sitting nearby.

'Mr Bateman, what did you ask Cathy to promise?' Tibbie Glencairn interrupted politely. 'It can't have been marriage — for you are already married, aren't you?'

For the first time since he set foot in the villa, Graham faltered.

Senora Ramis frowned at Tibbie's question.

'I'm in the process of getting a divorce,' he said defensively. 'Then Cathy and I can be married.'

'I've told you — I'm not going to marry you!' Cathy protested.

Senora Ramis stood up, her displeasure evident.

'Mr Bateman, you have deceived me. You led me to believe that you were Cathy's heartbroken fiancé, yet it seems that you are already married to someone else.' She gestured towards the door.

'I have no wish to be involved in your personal affairs. Please leave my house at once!'

'I was only doing what was best for you,' he told Cathy. 'But you had to have it all your own way, didn't you? Well, you'll regret this — I'll see to it!' He glowered at Cathy and strode out of the room.

Senora Ramis turned to Cathy. 'I want you to leave, too. Your services are no longer required. I will not risk my children being involved in any way with a man like that.'

'But I can't . . . ' Cathy said, her face pale. 'I've no money to pay for the flight home.'

'That is not my problem! Why don't you go with your boyfriend — he has a ticket for you!' Senora Ramis's voice was hostile. 'I do not want you to spend another night in my house!'

There was no point in arguing any further. Cathy turned and headed dazedly for her room, followed by Tibbie.

Tibbie Glencairn said nothing until they were alone.

'Cathy, what are you going to do

now?' she asked quietly.

'I've no idea. I've no money, nowhere to stay . . . oh, what a mess!' Cathy cried.

'Don't upset yourself, love,' Tibbie consoled her. 'Maybe you'll be better off away from Senora Ramis anyway. She's hardly an ideal employer. Look, why don't you come and stay with me for a while? It would give you a chance to sort yourself out.'

'Tibbie, it's very kind of you, but I don't want to impose on you . . . '

'Nonsense! But if you're worried about accepting charity, you can earn your keep! I've been thinking about advertising for a housekeeper for some time now. The job's yours if you want it!'

'Oh, thank you, Tibbie!' Cathy bit her lip to hold back the tears that threatened. 'You're such a good friend to me . . . '

'Not a bit of it!' Tibbie Glencairn said briskly. 'You'll have to work hard, mind. But if you still want the job, be as quick as you can about packing. I'm expecting guests this evening.'

It took just ten frantic minutes for Cathy to collect her belongings together. She was heaving her two suitcases out of the back door when Phillipe stopped her.

'This is not your fault! You shouldn't have to leave. I will speak to my sister,' he told her.

'No, thank you!' Cathy's voice was cold. 'I don't want to stay here after what your sister has said to me.'

'Then take this,' he said, holding out some money. 'It's not much, but it will be enough for you to live on until you find another job.'

Cathy was desperate to get away from the villa.

Phillipe was being very kind, but all she wanted was to blot out the last few hours.

She tried to smile politely at him.

'It's very kind of you, but I can't take your money. Please don't worry — I'm going to stay with Senora

Glencairn for a while.'

'I see.' Phillipe nodded. 'Will I see you again?' he pressed.

'Oh, I don't know.'

It was the last thing she wanted to think about at the moment.

'Look, Phillipe, I have to go now,' she insisted.

She could see Senora Ramis coming along the corridor and she couldn't face another confrontation.

'Then I will help you!' Phillipe seized her bags and set off purposefully down the drive.

Cathy stumbled after him, feeling completely powerless.

Tibbie Glencairn was waiting for her outside the apartment building. One glance at Cathy's ashen face made her take charge.

'Thank you, Phillipe. You can leave the cases here.' Tibbie smiled dismissively at the young man, ushering Cathy into the lift.

* * *

Later, after she'd had some tea in the soothing calm of Tibbie's lounge, Cathy's colour gradually returned.

'I'm really sorry about all this,' she apologised. 'I'll phone home and ask my parents to send out the money for my fare.'

'I thought you were going to take my job? I was being serious, you know. Look, I've already written out an advertisement.'

She handed Cathy a sheet of paper. 'It hasn't appeared in the newspaper yet, so if you want the job, it's yours.'

'Then I accept,' Cathy assured her.

She was too proud to go back to Glasgow with no job and no money.

'Don't you want to know what you'll be expected to do?' Tibbie laughed. 'It's all written down there!'

Cathy quickly read the advertisement. Housework was no problem for her — she'd lived in her own flat, after all. And her cooking was passable, if plain. She saw that she'd also be expected to travel with Tibbie as her companion.

'It all seems fine to me,' Cathy said, looking up with a smile.

'Good! It saves me the trouble of advertising, and all the business of interviewing.' The older woman seemed genuinely pleased.

'When do you want me to start?' Cathy asked.

'Now! I'm expecting a couple of old friends soon for a light supper — nothing too elaborate.' Tibbie Glencairn smiled. 'I've already made some sandwiches, so if you can finish the preparations I'll go and change into something a bit smarter.'

Cathy hurried through to the kitchen and set to work. As she buttered bread and chopped vegetables, she just couldn't stop thinking about the scene Graham had caused.

What had she ever seen in him? Now the very thought of him made her shudder with fear.

But there was no time to brood as

she raced to and fro, following Tibbie's instructions.

Cathy found herself dashing round the kitchen, trying to complete her tasks before the guests arrived.

'Now you go and change,' Tibbie told her briskly. 'Make yourself look smart. People here just love to gossip, so I want you to put on a brave face and prove to them that anything Senora Ramis says is wrong.'

⋆   ⋆   ⋆

I wish the doctor would tell me I was fit to drive again,' Tom muttered from the passenger seat.

He and Morag were driving through to Kilbarton to visit Gordon.

'Well, you don't really need the car just now, do you?' Morag smiled. 'Dad's keeping you busy in the office in the afternoons.'

'Hmm.' Tom frowned. 'You know, Nessie won't let me near that computer,' he complained. 'All I'm allowed to do is put stamps on envelopes!'

Tom was not pleased with his parents' suggestion that he should work in the office at Herald Motors until he was fully fit again.

He had little interest in office work, especially when he was given only trivial jobs to do. And he'd much preferred sitting with Aunt Olivia and Jemima in the afternoons, hearing stories about the family.

'Morag, before we go into Kilbarton, could we have a look at the site of the garage and see what's been done?' he asked suddenly.

'I suppose so.' Morag sighed, turning the car up the familiar side road.

They both gasped when they saw the 'For Sale' sign. They'd expected to see a cleared site, but their old bungalow was still standing, its windows boarded up. The garage buildings were still there, too.

'So it's true!' Tom said softly.

'Did you know the place was up for sale?' Morag asked in disbelief.

'One of the nurses at the hospital came from Kilbarton, and she told me there was talk that the property developers had gone bust. So I asked Gordon about it, and he confirmed that he'd heard the same thing.'

'He never mentioned it,' Morag complained. 'Why didn't you tell me?'

'I'm telling you now! Gordon wasn't sure if it was true. There have been so many rumours — first, they were going to build houses, then luxury flats. Some people were even talking about a new leisure centre.'

Tom stared at her.

'You've become very touchy since we moved to Aunt Olivia's. You used to be great fun when we lived here,' he told his sister wistfully before getting back into the car.

Morag stood for a few moments, watching him.

Tom's comments had touched a raw nerve, but she knew that he wouldn't say anything he didn't mean.

She remembered her outburst yesterday, when she'd accused Gordon of deliberately keeping secrets from her.

Had she allowed Cathy's problems to build up out of all proportion in her mind, making her irritable about almost everything else? She always seemed to be fretting about something these days.

Tom was sitting in the passenger seat, staring blankly out of the window, when she got into the car.

Morag felt suddenly downcast, and she looked back wistfully at her old home and the garage where she'd worked.

It seemed like a lifetime away — it was almost as if she was another person now that she was working in Glasgow.

'I wish we could come back here to live, and have everything the way it used to be,' Tom mumbled.

'We couldn't afford to buy it.' Morag sighed. 'And even if we could, things wouldn't be the same. Too much has happened to us.'

She started the car, and they drove in silence to Gordon's yard.

The rental cars and wedding limousines were parked in front of the office, all shining in the late evening sunshine. Peggy, who had worked in the shop at their old garage, hurried out to meet them.

Gordon McEwan had given her a job when the business closed down.

'Tom, you poor soul! How are you feeling now?' she asked.

'Oh, not so bad! I'll soon be back playing for Kilbarton Athletic again!' He pulled himself out of the car with his crutches and set off across the yard to the office.

Morag sat in the car for a moment, feeling slightly snubbed, as Peggy, still talking, hurried after Tom.

She pushed the thought aside in dismay.

The old Morag would never have felt hurt just because Peggy paid more attention to Tom than herself.

Morag got out of the car and looked down the line of rental vehicles. A burgundy-coloured Daimler had pride of place.

'How do you like the latest addition to my fleet?' She hadn't heard Gordon come up behind her. 'I bought it from one of Olivia's contacts.'

'It's beautiful,' Morag told him truthfully.

'I've moved this lot round to the front of the yard, so that I can keep the veteran cars under cover,' he explained.

★ ★ ★

Morag listened, absorbed, as he went on to describe all the improvements he wanted to make. For now at least, the awkwardness between them had disappeared.

Was it because she was back on home ground, she wondered?

'Here, let me have a look at you,' Peggy cried, when Morag walked into the office a little later. 'You're looking so glamorous these days!'

Morag smiled, a little embarrassed by the flattery.

'But are you sure you're not overdoing the dieting?' Peggy went on, suddenly concerned. 'You're so thin — and you look tired, too, love.'

'It's the worrying about Cathy that's done it,' Tom said lightly. 'Gordon, it's true about our old place,' he continued. 'We stopped to have a look on our way here, and there's a 'For Sale' sign up.'

'It must have just gone up, then. It wasn't there when I passed this afternoon,' Gordon remarked.

'Would you think of making an offer for the place?' Tom asked eagerly.

'Hang on a minute!' Gordon laughed at Tom's enthusiasm. 'I couldn't afford that kind of outlay.'

'I suppose not!' Tom sighed despondently.

He brightened up when another thought came to him. 'I wonder if Aunt Olivia would be interested?'

Peggy gasped.

'Don't even mention it to her!' she

warned. 'It would break your mother's heart if that woman got her house.'

'But they're all friends now!' Tom protested.

'Rubbish! I know for a fact that your mum and dad are only making the best of things. That woman treated them shamefully when they were first married . . . ' Peggy swept on.

'Come out into the yard and I'll explain all my plans to you,' Gordon interrupted quickly to divert Tom. He beckoned to Morag to go with them.

She took comfort from the way Gordon put his hand under her elbow to guide her gently around the yard. It was just like old times.

Their tour of the yard was interrupted by the arrival of Lorna and Max.

'Your mum said we'd find you here,' Lorna called to Morag. 'You'll never guess what I've just heard . . . '

' . . . that our old garage is up for sale,' Tom finished, delighted at stealing Lorna's thunder.

'We saw the 'For Sale' sign on our way here,' Morag explained. 'Now, let me see your ring!'

The two young women stood admiring the sparkling diamond on Lorna's engagement finger.

'Come on, Morag, let's go in and show it to Peggy, or I'll never hear the end of it,' Lorna said.

They left the three men in the yard and went into the small office, where Peggy was manning the radio control for the taxis.

She was delighted to be shown Lorna's ring, and even more delighted to hear that the wedding would be in September.

Morag enjoyed the next hour and relaxed in the familiar atmosphere.

She was reluctant to leave and drive back to Glasgow.

'Oh, Peggy, Aunt Olivia told me to invite you to the Silver Wedding celebrations on Saturday,' Tom remembered.

'That's kind of her,' Peggy said. 'It'll

be lovely to see everyone again.'

'I'm not sure how Mum and Dad are going to feel about this party,' Morag said quietly to Peggy, when Tom was out of earshot. 'They'd planned to go out for a quiet meal together next Tuesday, which is the actual date of their anniversary.'

'I'm sure they won't mind once they discover that Tom's done most of the organising,' Gordon commented.

He walked out to the car with Morag and bent down at the window to say goodbye as she took her place behind the wheel.

'You know, you haven't mentioned Cathy at all tonight!' he teased.

Morag stared down at her hands, wounded by Gordon's casual remark. She knew it was only meant lightly, but it hurt all the same.

'I'm still very concerned about her,' she replied coldly. 'You do realise that Graham Bateman will be in Majorca by now, don't you?'

Without waiting for Gordon's answer,

she started the car and drove off.

Was there something strange about her because she cared for her sister?

It seemed she couldn't win with Gordon — he criticised her if she spoke about Cathy, and reproached her when she didn't.

'So that's Lorna engaged,' Tom remarked lightly. 'When are you and Gordon planning to tie the knot?'

'Somehow I can't see that ever happening!' Morag snapped.

★   ★   ★

That Saturday afternoon, Helen and Simon Kinloch stood on the same spot as their son and daughter had done several days before. They gazed sadly at their old home.

'Morag did say it would upset us,' Helen murmured emotionally. 'But I didn't expect this.'

Simon took a bunch of keys from his pocket.

'I kept this set for sentimental

reasons. Let's see if they still fit.'

He walked over to the door, then beckoned to Helen.

'Come on, it won't do any harm. I just want to have a look.'

They walked from room to room in silence.

Helen felt near to tears to see how neglected this place she'd cherished for so many years had become.

'It isn't the home we left, is it?' Simon said, locking the door behind them, and looking at her thoughtfully.

'Let's have a look at the garage and workshop while we're here,' he suggested quietly.

For the next half-hour they wandered round the buildings.

From time to time Simon called out, pleased to have found certain items.

Helen said nothing, saddened by the derelict state of her former home. It was almost worse, in a sense, than seeing it bulldozed.

'How do you feel about us trying to buy it back?' Simon asked suddenly. 'I could commute to Glasgow each day, you would have your old home again, and Tom could run the garage here.'

He glanced down at Helen's smooth dark head bent over her hands, and waited for her reply.

After a little she raised her head.

'It would be a huge undertaking. For a start, it would mean a big bank loan. Then there's the house — it's only a shell now, and the garage buildings need repairing, too.' She sighed.

'And is it fair to tie Tom down? He might not want to work in a garage for ever.'

It wasn't the answer Simon had hoped for. He turned and looked into Helen's concerned brown eyes, his lips set in a tight line.

'I thought you'd be delighted to come back and live here,' he protested. 'I know you hate staying with Olivia.'

'Strangely enough, I don't! The only thing that bothers me is Olivia interfering in our lives. I don't like her manipulating Tom and finding Morag a job in her bridal salon. Now she's turned her attention to Gordon.'

'I don't see what you're so worried about. Tom's in the office with you every afternoon, away from her influence,' he replied quite reasonably. 'Anyway, Olivia's kept her word — she certainly hasn't interfered with the way I'm running Herald Motors. And the business venture she's offered Gordon is a sound one.'

'It's just that I have this image of us as her puppets, while she pulls the strings,' Helen explained. 'Maybe I'm being blinkered, but I find it hard to believe that Olivia has changed so much. She treated us so unfairly when we got married.'

'That was twenty-five years ago,' Simon reminded her gently.

Helen smiled to herself. She'd said the same thing to him when Olivia Kinloch first offered him the job.

'Will you at least consider my suggestion?' Simon asked.

She nodded, but as she looked

towards the boarded-up bungalow and weed-choked garden, her heart was heavy. This didn't feel like home to her any more, and she couldn't see herself living here again. Too much had happened for her to be able to go back.

'It's good of Olivia to invite us for dinner tonight to celebrate our anniversary,' Simon remarked as they drove back to Glasgow.

'Yes, it is. And Morag's given me such a lovely dress.' Helen smiled. 'She rushed the alteration through so that I could wear it this evening.'

Helen had arranged to meet Morag at the bridal salon to collect her new dress when they got back. They arrived just after closing time.

'Try it on now, Mum,' Morag urged, handing Helen the dress. 'We'd better make sure it fits.'

Simon gasped in admiration when Helen appeared in the fitted silk dress. Her newly-cut dark bob made her look twenty years younger.

'I'll have to watch the young men

when I have a wife who looks like this,' he tried to joke, but his voice was husky with emotion.

Morag watched her parents, envying their close relationship.

Would she and Gordon ever get to this stage? She had no idea where she stood with him — or how he felt about her.

It was nearly seven when they arrived home.

Morag had managed to persuade her mother to keep the new dress on, and she hoped they wouldn't notice the familiar cars parked nearby.

Jemima was waiting for them.

'I don't know why Olivia had to get caterers in. I could have managed,' she grumbled as she ushered them towards the door of the drawing-room. As she opened it, a loud cheer greeted them.

Helen and Simon watched in disbelief as all their oldest friends surged forward to wish them well.

White-aproned waitresses appeared with glasses of champagne, and Tom came in, pushing his aunt in a wheelchair.

'Could we have some quiet, please?' Tom called. 'Has everyone got a full glass? We're about to propose a toast.'

Olivia Kinloch took a glassful of champagne from the tray that was held out to her. 'Let's drink to Helen and Simon, who have made their twenty-five years of marriage such a wonderful success story.' She raised her glass. 'To Helen and Simon!'

There was an outburst of cheering and clapping as everyone repeated the toast.

Helen and Simon stood, bewildered, trying to take in what was happening.

'I hope you like it! I told Aunt Olivia who to invite.' Tom grinned at them both.

'I wanted to do something to thank you for forgiving me,' Olivia Kinloch said quietly. 'Having you and your family here means so much to me.'

'Thank you.' Helen felt a little

ashamed that she still couldn't bring herself to warm to her sister-in-law. That would take more time . . .

But she was glad to see Simon bend down and kiss his sister's cheek. It was right that they should make up their differences.

Lorna tapped Morag on the shoulder.

'Gordon phoned a little while ago — he's been delayed, but he'll be here soon,' she said.

'He's working late again, I suppose,' Morag murmured.

'No, he was quite mysterious . . . ' Lorna started to explain, but she was interrupted by an old friend who wanted to congratulate her on her engagement.

The guests soon started to drift towards the buffet that had been laid out in the dining-room.

Morag stayed in her place by the window, watching for Gordon.

It was almost an hour later when his car pulled up outside the house.

Then the front door opened, and she gasped in disbelief. There, on Gordon's arm, was a smiling and radiant Cathy.

Too Tired To Care

Morag was amazed by how carefree Cathy seemed. She was flitting around the room, chatting and laughing with the guests. It was as if the events of the past few weeks had never happened.

'I can't believe Cathy's here. She looks so well — you'd never know how much trouble Graham Bateman caused her.'

Morag shook her head in disbelief.

'She's lucky to have found such a sympathetic new employer as Tibbie Glencairn. When she heard about the silver wedding celebration she brought forward a meeting in London and arranged for Cathy to fly up here,' Gordon told her.

Morag wondered how he knew so much about Cathy — and why he and Cathy had arrived at the party together.

Surely there wasn't something going

on between the two of them?

She didn't have the energy to ask him about it. She'd had a persistent headache recently. It had worsened since this morning, when she and the salon assistant, Lorraine, had had words.

Lorraine's latest boyfriend who was unemployed had started hanging about the shop for most of the day, and Morag had asked him to leave.

Lorraine had been furious.

Now Morag was watching for an opportunity to ask Aunt Olivia how she should deal with the situation.

'How about getting something to eat?' Gordon suggested.

'Yes, fine . . . oh, hang on a minute, Gordon,' she said apologetically. 'I need to speak to Aunt Olivia.'

Morag hurried over to her aunt, who was on her own for the first time that evening.

'This is the first opportunity I've had to speak to you all night — you've been so busy,' Morag said with a smile.

'It's going well, isn't it?' Olivia said happily. 'It was a lovely surprise to see Cathy, too. And your parents seem to be enjoying themselves — I've never seen your mother smile so much!'

Morag nodded in agreement. She, too, had noticed how relaxed and happy Helen was — Cathy's arrival had cheered everyone up.

But now she had to tell her aunt about the disagreement she'd had with Lorraine.

Worse still, she would have to let Olivia know that Lorraine had marched out of the shop in the middle of the afternoon.

'It's my fault,' Olivia said with a sigh, when Morag had finished. 'I should have made it clear to Lorraine from the start that you were in charge.

'As to what you should do now — ' she paused, tapping her fingers on the arm of her wheelchair ' — I think you should wait and see what happens. If Lorraine doesn't come in on Monday, then she's dismissed herself.

'I've got a feeling, though, that she'll be back. She's too smart to throw away such a good job because of a trivial argument.'

'You're right.' Morag smiled. 'Thanks for the advice.'

'Don't let these things worry you.' Olivia Kinloch looked closely at her niece. 'You're very pale, Morag. Are you feeling all right?'

'I've just got a bit of a headache.' Morag dismissed it lightly, but the truth was she'd felt under the weather for some time. Her chest felt tight and sometimes she was finding it hard to breathe.

'Would you like to go through to the buffet?' she asked, forcing herself to be cheerful.

'Yes, please. Gordon, could you help with my wheelchair?' Olivia called to him, and he came over to them, smiling.

Gordon and Olivia were soon discussing vintage cars.

Morag was relieved just to sit in a

corner and listen. It was all she had the energy for at the moment.

She was feeling increasingly unwell, and concentrating was difficult. She had no appetite and pushed her plate away, untouched. She looked around, thinking that all she wanted was to escape from the noise and the crowds, and get to bed just as soon as she could.

'Morag, do you think you could help me through to bed?' Olivia asked a little later. 'I'm so tired all of a sudden.'

Morag forced herself up from her chair, feeling extremely unsteady on her feet. Somehow, she managed to push the wheelchair through to Olivia's room and helped her aunt to undress.

Within five minutes Olivia was in bed. She lay back against the pillow, looking suddenly frail and exhausted.

'I'm so glad to have seen this night,' she whispered. 'I'm a very happy woman, Morag. I've finally been able to do something to right a wrong. You've no idea how much that means to me.'

* ★ *

Gordon was waiting for Morag outside Olivia's door.

'Morag, can we talk?' he began, but she didn't seem to hear him.

'Look, Gordon!' She clutched at his arm, looking across the room. 'There's Jamie Stewart with Cathy! Oh, I do hope they can work things out.' She smiled. 'That would be wonderful!'

Lorna's younger brother was standing stiffly beside Cathy, who was talking intently.

Morag suddenly remembered the last time she'd seen them together, at Lorna's cheese and wine party. Cathy had been the silent one then, and Jamie had been trying to gain her interest.

Of course, so much had changed since then . . .

As the guests started to leave, Morag helped Jemima to find their coats.

She felt as if she was operating on automatic pilot as she helped people into their coats, escorted them to the door and waved them off.

Gordon was one of the last to leave.

'I don't think you've heard half of what I've said tonight,' he complained.

'I know — I'm sorry. I'm not quite with it.' She shook her head.

He looked at her as if it was a poor excuse.

'You looked lovely tonight. Maybe old friends like me are a little dull for you these days.' He gave her a peck on the cheek and left.

At last, everyone had gone, and the Kinlochs found themselves alone amidst the debris of the party.

'Well, everyone seemed to have a good time!' Tom declared.

'I'm so glad I was able to come home,' Cathy said. 'You made a good job of organising things, Tom.'

'Your mother and I really appreciated it.' Simon Kinloch patted his son affectionately on the shoulder.

'And it was a real treat to have you here, love,' he said to Cathy. 'It's a pity you have to go away again so soon.'

'I wish I could stay longer, Dad,' Cathy told him, 'but I have to meet Tibbie in London tomorrow morning.' She turned to her sister with a smile.

'Morag, could you give me a lift to the airport in the morning? I'm booked on the first shuttle.'

Morag nodded, hoping desperately that she would feel better by then. She left the rest of the family discussing the events of the evening and stumbled up to bed. She was just drifting off to sleep when the door opened and Cathy came in.

'Morag, are you asleep?' she whispered.

Morag forced her eyelids open and sat up.

'Well, I was. I'm pretty tired, Cathy. It's a pity your plane is so early in the morning — I've hardly seen you.'

'I suppose I could get a later one, but I'm terrified that Graham might find out I'm in Glasgow. I really don't want to bump into him.' Cathy shrugged.

'Did you want to talk to me?' Morag

asked, stifling a yawn. 'Only it's getting late . . . '

'Oh, Morag, it's Jamie!' Cathy blurted out. 'I really hurt him by running off to Majorca like that, and he hasn't forgiven me. He was so polite and cold with me tonight. I've ruined everything!'

Tears glittered in Cathy's eyes as she settled herself down on the edge of the bed. 'Lorna was very unfriendly, too. If Gordon hadn't been so kind and encouraging, I don't think I'd have had the courage to walk into the party tonight.'

Morag listened sympathetically, wishing she could summon up the energy to comfort her sister.

'I thought that when I saw Jamie and explained about Graham Bateman, he'd understand. But he didn't even want to listen to what I had to say.

'I really envy you having someone like Gordon, Morag.' Cathy sighed. 'He's so dependable.'

'Jamie's been hurt — it'll take time

before he can forgive you,' Morag said, too tired to talk any more.

'It's late, and we both have to be up early tomorrow. Good-night, Cathy.' She pulled the duvet up under her chin and turned over. She was past sleeping now.

Did she really have Gordon, she wondered? They always seemed to be at cross purposes these days.

★   ★   ★

Mrs Kinloch, thank you for a lovely party. I can't remember when I last enjoyed myself so much,' Nessie Louden said on Monday morning. She and Helen were catching up on some filing in the office.

'It's such a relief that the extra security is paying off,' Nessie went on, changing tack. 'We didn't lose any stock at all last week.'

'It's an improvement,' Helen Kinloch agreed. 'But our margin of profit isn't what it should be.'

The door of the office banged suddenly, making them both jump, as Tom came in.

'I could take a look at the computer records, to try to find out what the problem is,' he offered. 'I was pretty good on the computers at school.'

Nessie looked uncomfortable. In the last week Tom had run rings round her, showing her things she'd never realised the computer could do.

'I don't think that would work, Tom,' she ventured. 'The computer is in use all day.'

'Then I'll come in with Dad in the morning, and get an hour's work done before the office opens.' Tom grinned.

He was suddenly finding the office side of the business surprisingly fascinating.

Helen was anxious to encourage her son's interest in the administration of the business.

'I don't see what harm it would do,' she said.

'Well, if you're sure, Mrs Kinloch,'

Nessie conceded.

There was a knock at the door and Michael McQuade came in. He handed Tom an old, oil-covered manual.

'That's for the Model-T Ford,' he said.

'Thanks!' Tom took the book carefully. 'Don't worry — I'll take good care of it.'

'Good! It's seventy years old and irreplaceable.'

Tom looked down at the tattered book in his hand, suddenly wary. Then his face brightened.

'I know what I'll do — I'll photocopy it when I'm in before the office is open.'

'You'll be busy! All your spare time will be taken up with the computer, the photocopier — not to mention repairing the Model-T Ford!' Helen laughed.

'And I'll have to find time for football training in another few weeks. My leg should be strong enough by then.' Tom grinned, unaware of the flicker of anxiety on his mother's face.

'You'll have to do as the doctor tells

you,' she cautioned.

'If you want any pieces of the old Ford repaired, or even new bits made, we'll try to help in the repair shop. It's good practice for the apprentices,' Michael offered.

The phone interrupted them and Nessie answered it.

'It's for you,' she told Helen. 'Someone called Lorraine.'

Helen took the receiver, then frowned.

'I'll come right away,' she said, putting the phone down.

'Nessie, I have to go. Morag's not well — she's fainted in the shop.'

'Morag's never ill,' Tom put in. 'Do you want me to come with you?'

'No, you stay here and tell Dad where I've gone. He's in the showroom.'

It didn't take long for Helen Kinloch to reach the bridal salon where she found Morag sitting in the office, looking very pale and drawn.

'One minute she was speaking to me, and the next she was on the floor,' Lorraine said anxiously.

'I'll be fine!' Morag protested weakly. She hated all these people fussing around her.

'Morag, you need to see a doctor. You've been sickening for this all weekend. Come on, I'm taking you home,' Helen insisted, and with Lorraine's help she got Morag out to the car.

In minutes they were home.

Morag stumbled into the hall and gazed up at the red-carpeted flight of stairs in front of her.

Suddenly, she felt incapable of climbing up to her room in the attic, or even moving. She sank down heavily on to the first step.

Helen called to Jemima to help her, and together the two women supported Morag through to the little back room where Tom had slept while he was still using crutches.

*   *   *

When the doctor arrived Morag was running a very high temperature. He made his diagnosis quickly.

'It's pneumonia,' he told Helen. 'And for it to have got to this stage, I'd say the virus has been working on Morag for some time.' He smiled encouragingly. 'But we can cure it now within days, you know.'

He took his prescription pad from his inside pocket.

'Hasn't she complained about feeling ill?' he asked Helen quietly.

Helen tried to think back.

'She did say something about a slight headache,' she remembered. 'But Morag hates to cause a fuss. She doesn't often complain about feeling ill — she just carries on.'

Looking back, Helen Kinloch felt a pang of guilt. They'd all been so busy with the celebrations for the silver wedding anniversary that they'd hardly given Morag a minute's thought.

Then there had been Cathy's unexpected visit . . .

Helen had been so excited to see her younger daughter that she'd had little sympathy for Morag's headache. And then they'd allowed Morag to drive Cathy to the airport when she must have been feeling terrible . . .

'Try to get these as soon as possible.' The doctor handed Helen a prescription. 'She should take them every four hours until the bottle is finished. I'll call in again tomorrow to see how she's doing.'

The next week passed in a haze for Morag. She was aware of people coming into her room and asking how she was feeling, but she had no idea of how quickly or slowly time was passing.

She was very grateful to Olivia and Jemima, for they seemed to be constantly by her bedside. It was comforting to know that there was always someone close at hand.

But as the drugs began to work, she became more aware of her surroundings. She soon realised that Gordon McEwan hadn't visited her, and she felt disappointed.

Lorna hadn't called, either. When

Helen next looked into her room, Morag broached the subject.

'You must be feeling better, if you're fretting about things like that.'

Helen pointed to a large vase of flowers on the bedside table.

'Gordon sent these, and Lorna and Max brought that plant. Don't you remember their visit?'

Morag shook her head, then remembered that she'd agreed to have dinner with her three friends on the previous Saturday evening.

Her mother seemed to read her thoughts. 'Don't worry — Lorna says she'll arrange another date for dinner when you're feeling better.'

Morag lay back on her pillows, wondering when that would be.

By the end of the second week of her illness, she was determined to make an attempt to get up, and she walked the short distance to her aunt's room.

By the time she got there, perspiration beaded her forehead, and she was gasping for breath.

'Go back to bed. You shouldn't be up yet,' Olivia scolded her.

Morag gratefully returned to her room.

It was another two weeks before she felt strong enough to get dressed and stay up for the afternoon.

It was still a relief to her to get back to bed and lie listlessly, uninterested in the comings and going of the household.

Gordon visited several times, and chatted to her about how his business was doing. Morag was glad that he seemed content to do the talking. Even holding a conversation exhausted her for hours.

★   ★   ★

One evening, Morag was sitting quietly in her room when her mother and father came in together.

'What are you doing, sitting here all by yourself? There's a good film on TV,' Simon Kinloch said lightly, but his eyes were concerned.

He sat down on the bed beside Morag. 'Your mother and I have been having a talk,' he said gently. 'We think you could do with a holiday — somewhere sunny, where you can relax and get your strength back. What do you think?'

'I'm fine — just a bit tired, that's all,' Morag assured him.

'That's not all! You're exhausted and you need a break!' Helen told her. 'And the doctor agrees.'

'Cathy phoned this morning with a suggestion,' Simon went on. 'Mrs Glencairn is going away on business for a month, and she's invited you to stay in her apartment in Majorca to keep Cathy company.'

Morag closed her eyes.

At the moment she found it tiring simply to stay in her bedroom all day. She didn't feel capable of travelling abroad for the first time.

'Dad, I couldn't . . . ' she began. 'I'd have to book tickets, and . . . '

'Don't worry about it, love. We'll make all the arrangements for you,' Simon reassured her. 'And Cathy will meet you off the plane in Majorca.'

'But I don't think I really want to go,' Morag protested quietly.

Helen and Simon exchanged worried glances.

This wasn't like Morag at all.

Her illness seemed to have changed her completely. They were sure that a holiday in the sun, away from all the pressures of day-to-day life, would do her good.

Morag tried to voice her objections several times over the next few days, but her family were so keen for her to go that she finally gave up.

She took little interest in the trip as the arrangements were made.

Helen Kinloch packed Morag's suitcase for her on the afternoon before she was due to leave.

'I'm sorry to be causing you all this trouble,' Morag said guiltily, noticing the worried look on her mother's face.

'Don't be daft,' Helen retorted. 'It's not your fault that you're ill. Anyway,' she went on, sitting down on the bed, 'some good's come out of it all. Your dad's been so concerned about you that he's dropped the idea of buying back the business in Kilbarton.

'I'm so relieved — he'll be retiring in ten years, and the last thing he should be doing is taking on a huge debt.'

Suddenly, they heard footsteps on the stairs, followed by the sound of Tom's bedroom door being slammed.

The two women looked up to see Simon standing in the doorway.

'What are you doing here? Have you decided to give yourself a day off?' Helen asked lightly, but Simon Kinloch frowned.

'I've been to the hospital with Tom,' Simon told her. 'We were all so worried about Morag that we almost forgot his check-up appointment.'

'What's wrong? What did the doctor say?' Helen demanded.

'Tom's leg is fine — it's healed

perfectly,' Simon revealed. 'But the doctor is not so happy with the progress of his head injury.' He paused, looking from his wife to his daughter. 'He's been advised not to play football, or any other physical contact sport. The doctor thinks that another such blow to his head could prove fatal!'

Gordon Might Phone . . .

Simon Kinloch stopped in the middle of adjusting his tie and turned slowly to his wife.

'Helen, just for tonight, do you think we could forget our children and their problems? It's time we started thinking about each other.'

Helen stared at him. She'd had so much to worry about lately that she'd neglected Simon, she knew. But her family had needed her . . .

'I'm sorry,' she apologised, smiling up at him. 'Has it really been so awful?'

'Of course not,' Simon said. 'I've been worried, too. But our children are grown up now. We can't solve all their problems for them, however much we want to.'

'I know.' Helen sighed. 'But Cathy's so far away — and Tom's devastated about not being able to play football. As for Morag — she's just getting over her illness. How are we going to tell her about that terrible fire at Gordon's garage?'

Simon shook his head, recalling the visit they'd had earlier in the week from a shocked Gordon McEwan.

'Poor Gordon,' Simon said sadly. 'He lost all his vintage cars in that blaze — what a tragedy. They're irreplaceable, no matter how well insured he was. But he saved his taxi fleet. That's one blessing.'

He reached out for Helen and hugged her close.

The fire which had destroyed his garage was a horrific blow for Gordon. But he was determined to build his business up again, and he was already piecing together what could be salvaged.

'We can't do any more to help,' Simon pointed out. 'Let's try to enjoy ourselves tonight — this is our own private celebration of our anniversary, remember!'

'You're right,' Helen agreed. 'And I'm not going to let Tom's bad mood bother me any more!'

Since Tom had been told that he couldn't play football because of his head injury he'd been impossible to live with.

'He's certainly made sure we all know how fed-up he is,' Simon put in.

'It's Olivia and Jemima I feel sorry for,' Helen said. 'He hasn't spoken to either of them for days.'

She would never have believed she could feel pity for her sister-in-law, but she'd seen how hurt Olivia was by Tom's sulky behaviour.

Helen finished dressing and put the last touches to her make-up.

'How do I look?' she asked, turning to Simon.

'Wonderful,' he said slowly. 'Absolutely wonderful.'

He took a faded velvet-covered box from the inside pocket of his jacket.

'This is for you,' he said, handing it to Helen. 'These were my mother's. She wanted my wife to have them one day.'

Helen took the box and opened it hesitantly. Inside was an old-fashioned string of pearls with an antique clasp, and a pair of earrings to match.

Helen stared at them for a few minutes.

Simon's mother had died when he was a baby, so Olivia must have given them to him.

'Don't you like them?' he asked, concerned.

'They're beautiful . . . and since they were your mother's, I'll be honoured to wear them.'

He frowned, a little put out by the stilted way in which she'd accepted his gift. He had thought she would be pleased.

Helen sensed his disappointment.

She knew she was over-sensitive about Olivia's involvement, but she couldn't help it. She still resented her sister-in-law . . .

She lifted the earrings from the box and clipped them on to her ears. Then she held the necklace out to Simon.

'Would you help me to put this on?'

'Of course. You like them, don't you? My mother gave them to Jemima before she died, with the instruction that they were to be given to my wife one day.' He sighed suddenly.

'Out of loyalty to Olivia, Jemima didn't hand them over when we got married,' he explained.

Helen stood in front of the mirror to admire the beautiful jewellery, turning this way and that for the best effect in the light.

'So at last, after twenty-five years, I'm acknowledged as your wife.'

Helen laughed softly, still regarding herself in the mirror, relieved that his sister had had no hand in the matter.

Olivia seemed to reach into every corner of the family's affairs.

'They really are beautiful,' she said, fingering the pearls. 'Thank you.'

Suddenly, the mirror in front of her swayed as a door above them slammed.

'He's gone too far!' Simon said

angrily, rushing out of the door.

'Simon, don't — Tom's got a lot on his mind just now ... ' Helen's voice tailed off as Simon pounded up the stairs to Tom's bedroom.

She crossed to the door and opened it quietly.

She could hear Simon angrily telling Tom off, and Tom's equally furious voice answering back.

Soon Simon thundered back down the attic stairs.

He glared at Helen, then saw how much the argument had upset her.

'Tom has to learn that he's not the only person in the world with problems!' he blurted out.

'There's a lot worse off than him, too. And he can't just take his bad temper out on the rest of us. It's got to stop!'

'You're right, dear,' Helen agreed quietly, but she wished Simon hadn't been so hard on Tom.

She stood in front of Simon and took his hand in hers.

'We'll still have a wonderful evening, I promise. And Tom will soon apologise, I'm sure. He doesn't bear grudges.'

She stood on tip-toe and kissed him lightly on the cheek.

At once she felt him relax, and he laughed.

'The truth is, he gave as good as he got when . . . '

A tap on the door interrupted him, and they glanced at each other.

Then the door opened and Tom walked in. He stood awkwardly just inside the room, trying to meet his father's eye.

'I've come to apologise, Dad,' he mumbled. 'I didn't mean to slam the door. The window was open and the draught caught the door . . . but I shouldn't have said what I said.'

'Neither should I!' Simon held out his hand. 'I went a bit over the top.'

'Thanks!' Tom tried to smile. 'Well, that's all I wanted to say. Have a nice evening.' He turned dejectedly to go out.

Helen clasped her hands tightly together, desperately wanting to comfort him.

'Why don't you come with us?' Simon asked impulsively.

'Are you sure you don't mind?' Tom glanced from Simon to Helen. 'That would be great. I've done enough brooding lately. It would be nice to get out of the house for a while.'

'You'll have to change into something smarter,' Helen told him.

'No problem! I'll be back in a minute!'

When Tom had gone, Helen turned to face her husband.

'Do you know, for all your blustering, you really are a big softie! And I love you for it!' she whispered, hugging him.

'Well, maybe that's what was needed to clear the air!'

⋆ ⋆ ⋆

It was late afternoon when Morag woke up. She'd dreamt that she was back in their garage at Kilbarton. Gordon had been there, waiting in the background as always.

Gradually, as her eyes blinked open, she became aware of the striped awning at the front of the terrace, gently billowing above her head.

She stared up at it for a few moments, enjoying the warmth of the Mediterranean sun on her skin.

It was her second week here, and at last she felt that her strength was returning. She swung her legs off the lounger and stood up. The view from Tibbie's balcony was spectacular.

Morag loved watching the procession of boats which passed to and fro beneath her — fishing boats with their deep-throated diesel engines, little one-man boats which crept close to the shore, and sleek speedboats zooming over the water.

'Good afternoon.'

She jumped at the unexpected sound of a male voice. A tall, fair-haired man in a casual shirt and pale cotton trousers was sitting at the table at the end of the terrace.

Morag looked round quickly for Cathy, but there was no sign of her.

She swallowed nervously.

'I'm Morag Kinloch,' she said, expecting him to introduce himself, but he just looked at her.

'Morag? Not Cathy?' he asked.

Morag felt a stab of anxiety.

If he didn't even know what Cathy looked like, how had he got into the flat?

She bit her lip, trying to decide what to do next.

'I'll go and find Cathy for you,' she said carefully. 'What name will I say?'

'Alan Glencairn.'

Morag paused.

'Mrs Glencairn isn't here at the moment. Are you related?'

'She's my mother. I usually stay here when I'm in Majorca.'

'Oh, I see! Then you must have a key to the apartment.'

'Yes, I do. It is my mother's

apartment, after all,' he said.

Morag flinched at the sarcasm in his remark. Then she remembered that Cathy had gone shopping.

She glanced at her watch. Cathy had been gone for two hours.

'My sister should be back shortly,' she told him.

Alan Glencairn didn't answer.

He picked up a pile of unopened mail from the hall table and flicked through it.

'Here's the letter I wrote to tell Mum I was coming. No wonder she didn't meet me at the airport — she hasn't opened it.'

'That's because she's in Belgium,' Morag pointed out.

'I thought she might be,' he muttered.

Morag wasn't sure what to do.

She was uncomfortably aware that she was a guest here, and that he had more right to be in Tibbie's apartment than she had.

'It's time for my swim,' she announced

with forced brightness, picking up her holdall.

She felt a real sense of freedom, when she reached the pool, which was deserted. Till now Cathy had gone everywhere with her, fussing about her health.

Morag changed quickly in one of the cubicles.

She disliked being continually mollycoddled, and she felt a little thrill of excitement at being strong enough to swim on her own.

★   ★   ★

The water was much colder than she'd expected, but she stood still for a moment and splashed herself, then slowly leaned forward and struck out for the other end.

She was doing well until, three-quarters of the way up the pool, she felt a surge of panic as tiredness dragged at her limbs.

She turned at once and floated on

her back, realising that she had to get to the ladder, which was about ten feet away.

She forced her arms and legs to propel her across to the metal handrail and clung on tightly, her head barely above the water.

She concentrated hard, summoning up the strength to climb each rung until she could heave herself on to the poolside.

She'd just managed to pull herself clear of the water when she heard Alan Glencairn's voice above her.

'I've been watching you for the last few minutes. Is there something wrong?'

Despite her exhaustion, exasperation surged through her. He'd seen she was in trouble, but he hadn't tried to help!

'Yes. Couldn't you see that I was having difficulty?' she managed to say through clenched teeth.

'Here, hold on.' He bent down and took her hands, then pulled her up the last few rungs.

She sank down to the ground,

gasping for breath.

'What's going on?' a voice called out.

Morag had never been so relieved to see her sister.

'Oh, Morag, you didn't try to swim on your own!' Cathy scolded.

'I thought I'd be fine. I did three lengths yesterday, but I couldn't even finish one today,' Morag said wearily.

'Cathy, this is Mrs Glencairn's son, Alan,' she went on, suddenly remembering the young man who'd helped her out of the pool.

She was relieved to be able to concentrate all her strength on standing up while Alan explained to Cathy that he'd expected his mother to be home.

Back upstairs in the bedroom they shared, Cathy bombarded Morag with questions about Alan Glencairn.

'Tibbie doesn't talk about him much,' Cathy told her sister. 'I got the feeling that things were slightly strained between them — but I could be wrong.'

'She doesn't know he's here. The letter saying that he was coming arrived after she'd left,' Morag said. 'Maybe you should let her know that he's here.'

'Yes, that's a good idea. She may not want him to sleep in her bedroom — she keeps a lot of personal stuff in there.'

As it turned out, Cathy didn't have to phone Tibbie.

When the sisters went back into the lounge they found Alan making up a bed on one of the loungers. Then he pulled out the glazed partition which slotted between the balcony and the terrace roof, transforming the terrace into a small room.

'This gives us all privacy,' he explained. 'I'd appreciate it if you'd leave these lounge curtains closed in the morning. I'll open them when I get up,' he said.

'I'm just about to make supper. Would you like some?' Cathy asked politely.

'Thanks. I haven't eaten since I was on the plane, so a meal would be welcome.' And he turned, closing the patio doors behind him, and disappeared on to the terrace.

'He obviously doesn't want our company.' Cathy frowned. 'I don't know what to make of him at all.'

The two sisters and Alan Glencairn were just about to sit down to their meal when the front entry buzzer sounded.

Cathy made to answer the internal phone, but Alan got there before her.

'Phillipe — what a surprise! Come on through — we're just about to eat, but I'm sure we can manage to feed another one . . . '

It was obvious from the way they greeted each other that Alan and Phillipe were good friends.

Cathy watched them, a little perturbed. She'd managed to avoid Phillipe since she'd starting working for Tibbie. He'd constantly pestered her to go out with him when she'd worked for his sister, Senora Ramis.

'We could always eat out!' Alan suggested suddenly.

Morag was surprised when Cathy immediately agreed with Alan's suggestion, for the meal they'd prepared was almost ready.

'That's two for going out — and I'm neutral,' Alan declared. 'The decision's yours, Morag.'

Morag was uneasy about having responsibility for the rest of the evening thrust open her.

'I was going to stay in . . . Gordon might phone, you see,' she explained, glancing at Cathy.

'Why should he?' Cathy's voice was unusually sharp.

Her parents had asked her to keep the news of the fire at Gordon's garage from Morag, so as not to upset her.

Morag said nothing.

Cathy didn't know that she'd sent Gordon a postcard with the phone number on and asked him to call her. She was concerned that she hadn't heard from him.

Very Suspicious

Helen Kinloch was very happy as she sat in the elegant dining-room of the country house hotel where they'd chosen to have dinner.

Morag and Cathy were both safe and well in Majorca, and Tom was beginning to get over his set-back. It looked as if their luck had changed for the better at last.

Later, when they'd finished their meal, Simon leaned back contentedly in his chair.

'That was wonderful!' he said.

'Brilliant!' Tom agreed. 'Wait a minute! Dad, look over there. It's Andy Davison — and that girl with him is . . . ' His voice tailed off as he tried to remember the name.

Simon and Helen looked over and watched as Andy Davison escorted a tall, slim girl to a table by the window.

'She seems very young,' Helen said doubtfully. 'Still, maybe she's a relative of his,' she added, trying to be charitable.

'I doubt it,' Simon said dryly. 'But, whoever she is, it's obvious that Andy Davison is a regular customer here. Look at how the waiters are fussing around him!'

Tom was silent as he watched the little scene across the room, and the girl in particular.

'That's no relative of Andy Davison's,' he announced. 'Her name is Louise Stevens, and she was in my class at school.'

His parents looked again, and Simon nodded his head slowly.

'You're right. Her parents ran the newsagent's in Kilbarton High Street. Larry Stevens used to buy his petrol from us.'

'Oh, I remember her now . . . '

Helen broke off in surprise as Louise Stevens suddenly caught sight of Tom and hurried across to their table.

'Hi, Tom!' She touched his hand. 'You're the last person I expected to see here!'

Then she turned quickly to Helen and Simon.

'It's nice to see you again, Mr and Mrs Kinloch. I work in Mr Davison's office now. We've been working late tonight, so he suggested we come out for something to eat.

'It's very grand here, isn't it?' she finished nervously. Then she smiled brightly.

'I'd better get back or Mr Davison will be wondering what's happened to me! Enjoy your meal!'

She glanced at Tom. 'I wish I was sitting here with you instead!' she said wistfully.

Andy Davison glared angrily at her as she returned to his table.

Then he looked across the room to the Kinlochs and gave them a half-hearted wave.

'I don't think he's too pleased to have been seen here with Louise,' Simon murmured, nodding to the waiter, who had brought the bill.

Simon glanced at it and raised his eyebrows.

'How can Andy afford to eat here regularly? Just look at these prices!'

'It's because he's a thief!' Tom blurted out.

Simon and Helen stared blankly at their son.

'Everybody at Herald Motors thinks he's the one who's been taking the stock,' Tom went on.

'Who's everybody?' Simon demanded.

'Michael McQuade and Nessie, for starters,' Tom told him. 'And Bertie, the storeman.'

'Then why haven't they told me?'

'Because they haven't any proof,' Tom said. 'But I'm pretty sure I can prove it. Come into the office with me tomorrow and I'll show you how I think he's done it.'

* * *

The atmosphere in the Herald Motors' office was tense as Michael McQuade, Bert, the storeman, and Nessie Louden, the secretary, stood together, considering the implications of what Simon Kinloch had just told them about the missing stores.

'It was Tom who worked it all out,' Simon went on. 'Andy Davison was taking our credit notes, and replacing them with forged ones.'

'But, Mr Kinloch, I always checked . . .' Nessie put in.

'It's OK, Nessie — none of this is your fault,' Simon reassured her.

'Andy Davison was clever, and he covered his tracks carefully. In fact, I don't see how we can prove any of this.' Simon sighed.

'But we can't let him get away with it! We've got to do something!' Michael McQuade burst out angrily. 'We could at least stop giving him a discount on the work we do for him.'

'That goes without saying! There's no way he'll get his five per cent. discount now!' Simon declared.

'But, Mr Kinloch — he gets a ten per cent. discount,' Nessie put in anxiously.

The three men stared at her, horrified.

'Miss Olivia wrote to me just before you started working here, Mr Kinloch. The letter said that Andy Davison's discount was now ten per cent. It was her signature, I'm sure.'

'Are you saying Olivia sent you . . . ' Simon started, but Nessie interrupted him.

'No, Andy Davison brought it.'

'Then we've got him! Olivia told me that his discount was five per cent.,' Simon said triumphantly.

'He must have forged the letter! Do you still have it?' he asked quietly.

'It's in here.' Nessie opened a drawer in the filing cabinet. 'I keep everything, you see.'

The three men watched expectantly as she flicked through the files.

'I don't know what's happened — it should be here,' she said in confusion, lifting out a folder. 'But I can't find it.'

Simon took the folder from her.

'You said you received the letter just before I started here — that would be March, then.'

He thumbed through the papers. Then he stopped, and showed everyone the open folder. It was obvious that a page had been torn out.

'So much for our only real piece of evidence,' he said glumly. 'No doubt Andy Davison removed it.'

They were interrupted by a tap on the office door.

Simon unlocked and opened it, and found Gordon standing there. 'I wanted to check whether it was OK to do some taxi repairs in the yard . . .'

He broke off, sensing that something was wrong.

'I'm sorry — am I interrupting something?'

Simon shook his head.

'No, we've just finished. Gordon, we know who's been stealing all the stock — it's Andy Davison. He's been so clever about it that we haven't any real proof to take to the police.'

'I see.' Gordon paused for a moment. 'Well, I can't say I'm surprised. He had quite a reputation with the taxi firms around here. He ran up a big bill with one firm, then moved on to another with no intention of paying the first.'

'He's a crook through and through!' Nessie said angrily.

'And there's nothing we can do about it!' Michael added dejectedly. 'Come on, Gordon — I'll get a working bay cleared for you.'

He shrugged hopelessly at Simon and pulled open the door to the yard.

Bert, the storeman, made to follow him out.

'It's just terrible!' he blurted out suddenly. 'Andy Davison's made fools out of us all — and we can't touch him . . . ' He went out to the yard, shaking his head.

Simon Kinloch lifted Nessie's coat from its hanger behind the office door.

'It's time you were off home, Nessie,' he said gently.

'Mr Kinloch, I'd work right through the night if it would help catch that man! And that letter did say ten per cent. I know it did!'

'I believe you.' Simon smiled. 'That's one good thing that's come out of all this mess. Everyone who works here has proved they're completely trustworthy. I won't forget it.'

Nessie gazed at him, lost for words. Then she smiled gratefully, gathered up her bag, and hurried out.

* * *

Simon turned to Gordon and noticed at once how tired he looked.

'Have you told Morag about the fire yet?' he asked.

Gordon shook his head.

'You two don't usually keep secrets from each other,' Simon remarked.

'I phoned late on Tuesday evening, but I didn't really get the chance to talk to her. There seemed to be a party going on in the flat,' Gordon explained.

'I see. Well, do try to tell Morag about the fire before she comes home. She'll be hurt if she finds out from someone else.'

Gordon nodded.

He'd been awake most of the night, thinking over all the things he'd wanted to say to Morag, but hadn't.

Tuesday's phone call hadn't been a success.

For a start, Morag hadn't given him her full attention.

He'd heard Alan Glencairn's voice in the background, calling her back to the party, and she'd seemed keen to finish the conversation and rejoin her friends.

He felt as if his dreams for himself and Morag had gone up in smoke, just like his business.

'I don't know where I stand with Morag these days,' Gordon told Simon. 'I've always hoped that, one day, we'd have a future together — but I'm not sure that she feels the same way.'

Gordon stopped, aware that he was expressing his feelings badly. But he was worried. There had never been anyone else for him but Morag and he'd planned that once he was able to offer her a secure future he'd ask her to marry him.

Once or twice over the last months, he'd tried to broach the subject, but he'd done so clumsily.

His attempts, however, just seemed to have driven them further apart.

'And now my business is back where it was five years ago.' Gordon shrugged. 'What do I have to offer her now?'

'You should be telling this to Morag, not me,' Simon Kinloch pointed out. 'I'm sure she'll understand.'

He sympathised with Gordon's dilemma, but he couldn't help thinking that his priorities were wrong.

It was good that Gordon wanted to build up a prosperous business — but surely he was wrong to put ambition before his courtship of Morag.

The door from the yard burst open

and Tom rushed in.

He stopped abruptly in his tracks when he saw how serious Simon and Gordon looked.

'What's up?' he asked.

'It's OK, Tom — come in. I've told everyone about Andy Davison, but we're still no further forward in finding any proof.'

'He'll go too far one of these days,' Gordon said. 'He's deceiving so many people that he's bound to be caught out.'

'I hope you're right.' Tom grinned. 'Gordon, I've got the old Ford Model-T in the workshop,' he went on. 'Would you mind taking a look at it? I'll do the repairs on your taxi for you.'

'How can I refuse an offer like that?' Gordon smiled at Simon. 'OK, Tom — it's a deal! It'll take my mind off other things.'

When the yard door closed behind them, Simon stood for a moment, enjoying the quietness of the office.

Then he picked up the phone.

He wanted to tell Helen about Andy Davison's latest deception.

★ ★ ★

Cathy stood by the edge of the pool, watching her sister doggedly swimming length after length.

At last Morag stopped. 'Twenty lengths today!' She gasped.

'That's good, but please don't do any more!' Cathy begged, holding out a towel. Her sister's stubborn determination to build up her strength alarmed her.

Morag climbed out and wrapped the bath sheet around her, rubbing her dripping hair with the end.

'I feel almost back to normal!' she said. 'I should be able to go back to work as soon as I get home next week.'

'You sound as if you're looking forward to leaving us,' Alan Glencairn said, pretending to sound hurt. 'Won't you miss me, Morag?'

'I'm glad to be going home — I feel so much better,' Morag declared brightly, dodging his question.

It was true.

Somehow, the weeks she'd spent in Majorca had put things into perspective for her.

When she was ill, everything had seemed hopelessly jumbled in her mind. But now, she could step back and look at her family's troubles more objectively.

'You'll walk away from me, Morag, without a backward glance!' Alan gave a mock love-lorn sigh.

'Yes, I will!' she replied tartly.

'You're so cruel!' he teased. 'I suppose you're going back to Scotland to break Gordon's heart, as you have mine!'

Cathy listened as Morag and Alan flirted with each other. They carried on like this all the time, and it seemed so out of character for Morag.

Cathy couldn't remember her ever being frivolous at home.

'I've got to go,' Morag announced. 'I'm expecting a phone call from Lorna. She wants to discuss her plans for the wedding.'

Morag wrapped a towelling robe round her slim, tanned body, and waved goodbye to Alan.

'You can't fool me,' he called after her. 'It's Gordon you're expecting to phone, not Lorna.'

'Well, you'll never know,' Morag quickly retaliated, without turning round.

Alan chuckled.

He looked across at Cathy, who was folding towels and packing bottles of sun lotion into a large holdall.

'Phillipe is arranging a picnic for the four of us up in the hills,' he remarked casually.

Cathy threw down the towel she was holding.

'I've already told Phillipe I'm not going on any more outings with him,' she said firmly.

'Whyever not?' Alan sounded surprised. 'He's a nice guy, he's good company, and he likes you a lot.'

'It's not as simple as that!'

Alan raised himself up on his elbow, and looked at her questioningly.

'Phillipe isn't in love with me,' she explained. 'I think he sees me as a challenge!'

She gave a bitter laugh.

'You see, to Phillipe I'm the British girl who fled to Majorca to escape a possessive, married boyfriend. I suppose he thinks that winning me over would be a real triumph of his charm.' She looked at him steadily. 'He probably imagines himself as some sort of romantic hero . . . '

She broke off, and there were a few moments of silence.

'I'm sorry,' Alan said quietly. 'I've been really tactless, haven't I?'

'It's not your fault. It all happened before you arrived.' Cathy sighed, sinking down on to the edge of his sun-lounger.

She stared at the sun sparkling on the smooth surface of the deserted pool, and tried to explain about Graham Bateman — how she'd been flattered at first by his interest, but had then become frightened.

The whole story poured out as Alan listened sympathetically.

'So that's why I object to Phillipe so much,' she finished. 'He's arrogant — too much like Graham. He does as he pleases, and ignores what I say.

'He arranges outings for the four of us, so that it's difficult for me to refuse. And I can't stand the way he's always trying to get me alone . . .'

'I can understand why you don't want Phillipe around.' Alan frowned.

'We could still go on the picnic — just you, me and Morag,' he suggested.

Cathy shook her head.

'I can't. Your mother is due home in two days, and there are things that I have to do before then. I've already put them off to go on the other outings.'

'Well, I can at least make sure that Phillipe doesn't bother you again.'

'I'd be very grateful,' Cathy thanked him.

She was relieved that she'd confided in Alan — he'd been so sympathetic.

She found Phillipe's persistence wearing, and it was good to know that she had an ally.

Alan wasn't as stern and unfriendly as she'd first thought.

Back in the apartment, Cathy was surprised to find Morag still sitting by the phone in her towelling robe. She looked very serious.

'Did you know about the fire in Gordon's garage a few weeks ago?' she asked at once.

'Oh, no! Lorna wasn't supposed to tell you!' Cathy cried in dismay.

'She didn't — but Peggy did,' Morag explained. 'She'd called into the surgery to collect a prescription while Lorna was on the phone to me. Lorna asked her if she'd like a word with me, and she told me about the fire.'

'I thought it was stupid to keep it from you.' Cathy frowned. 'But Mum and Dad didn't want to worry you.'

She looked anxiously at Morag.

'Don't worry! I'm just glad I know now,' Morag said. 'It explains why Gordon's been so strange with me lately. He's had so much on his mind.'

She glanced at her watch.

'I feel like a walk. I think I'll give him a call from the box on the hill. By the time I get there he should have arrived at the office.'

Cathy was relieved that Morag was taking the news so well.

Then her conscience told her that Morag knew Gordon would face up to his crisis.

He wouldn't run away from his problems, as she had done.

Now, looking back, she was ashamed of the way she'd deceived everyone.

But she still didn't know what else she could have done. She'd been desperate to escape from Graham Bateman. No-one knew how much the fear of him still haunted her.

* ★ ★

Gordon sat in his makeshift office amidst the blackened ruins of his garage.

He'd hoped to spend the rest of the day and evening catching up on the paper work that had accumulated recently.

But that had been before he received a phone call from Louise Stevens, the young Kilbarton girl who worked for Andy Davison.

Gordon frowned, recalling the jumbled story she'd told him. He'd decide what to do once he'd heard all the details from her, face to face.

He sighed in exasperation when the phone rang again.

This time it was Morag.

'What a surprise!' he said happily. 'It's great to hear from you. How are you feeling?'

Morag bit her lip and looked out from the phone box, high above the apartments.

The view over the sunny harbour, with its bobbing yachts and fishing boats, was like a painting.

It was hard to visualise Gordon sitting in his burnt-out garage buildings.

'Gordon, I know about the fire,' she said quietly.

'I see.' He took a deep breath. 'I was going to tell you, you know. I just didn't know how to.'

'I wish you'd told me. I found out from Peggy, of all people.'

Morag tried not to betray how hurt she felt.

'Worrying about Cathy made you ill,' Gordon pointed out. 'I didn't want to burden you with my problems just when you were getting better.'

'But part of the reason I couldn't cope with Cathy's problems was because I had no-one to talk to,' Morag retorted.

Then she stopped.

She'd wanted to sympathise with Gordon about the fire, but instead she

285

was nagging him.

Yet she was tired of being dismissed as weak and silly for caring about her sister.

And, sometimes, she was sure Gordon thought her illness stemmed solely from anxiety.

He seemed to forget that she'd had pneumonia.

'I'm sorry!' Gordon sighed. 'I should have been more supportive.'

'Oh, I'm sorry, too. I just wanted to phone and tell you how upset I am about the fire. It seems so unfair.'

'Thanks. I'm hoping I'll be able to build the business up again. But, to be honest, it'll take a few years to get back to where I was.'

He sounded so downcast that Morag wished suddenly she could reach out and touch him.

But so many miles separated them . . .

The flashing coin display on the payphone caught her eye.

'Gordon, I'm sorry, but I'll have to go. My money's run out . . . ' The line clicked and went dead.

Gordon stared down at his hand as he replaced the phone.

A deep surge of despair suddenly swept through him, and he buried his face in his hands.

He missed Morag so much.

The destruction of his business was nothing compared to the thought of losing her.

He looked up to see Louise Stevens standing nervously in front of his desk. He hadn't even heard her come in.

His concerns about Morag were soon forgotten as he listened to Louise's story.

'I met Mr and Mrs Kinloch and Tom last week, when they were out for dinner,' she explained. 'Tom hinted then that he didn't have a very high opinion of Mr Davison, so when I found some boxes belonging to Herald Motors in the warehouse I realised something was wrong.'

'Thanks for telling me,' Gordon said.

'I'll let Mr Kinloch know at once.'

He picked up the phone again and dialled the number.

Helen answered, and Gordon immediately told her Louise Stevens' story.

'So she's sure that some of our stock is in Andy Davison's warehouse?' Helen repeated. 'And he's been selling it on?'

'Louise says there are several boxes addressed to Herald Motors in the warehouse, but yours is only one of the firms involved. There's lots of other stuff there — sports equipment, children's clothes, even food and drink — and it's all being sold on a cash-only basis.'

'It sounds very suspicious.' Helen frowned. 'Gordon, I think we should call the police.'

'I'll bring Louise round now,' Gordon offered. 'She wants to tell you everything, face to face.'

When Gordon and Louise arrived at the house, Simon, Helen and Tom were waiting with Olivia Kinloch in her room.

Gordon allowed himself a wry smile when he saw the glitter of determination in Olivia's eye. Her body might be confined to a wheelchair, but her mind was as active as ever.

'Louise, have you told your parents any of this?' Simon asked gently, sorry to see how scared the girl looked.

'Yes, they know everything. It was my dad who suggested I should speak to Gordon first, to find out if there was a reason for Mr Davison having your stock.'

'Would you be willing to tell the police all this?' Olivia asked suddenly.

Louise nodded.

Olivia Kinloch turned to Simon and Helen.

'I think we should call them in. This whole thing is too serious for us to handle ourselves. Andy Davison is a criminal — and now we can prove it.'

'You do realise you'll lose your job over this?' Tom said, looking at Louise with concern.

'That's OK,' she said bravely. 'I've already decided I'm not going back. I don't want anything more to do with a man like that.'

Without any further hesitation, Simon Kinloch picked up the phone, and gave the details to the police.

No-one moved or said a word till he finished.

'It's out of our hands now,' he said grimly. 'But if Andy Davison knows Louise has seen his stolen goods, he'll have moved them by now. We could be too late!'

I've Always Loved You

It was a hazy early September morning when Morag Kinloch drove towards her old home town of Kilbarton.

She loved days like this, when the sun breaking through the cool mist brought the promise of a fine, warm day.

As she neared the side road which led up to her old home, she saw the 'For Sale' sign was still prominently displayed.

On impulse, she turned the car up the familiar road.

After the months she'd spent away, working in the bridal salon in Glasgow and then recuperating from her illness in Majorca, she was nostalgic for the view she'd once seen every day.

It was the only thing which was unchanged. The house was empty and had been badly vandalised, and the garage buildings were little better.

She swallowed as she saw once again the derelict bungalow, sitting in its tangled, weed-choked garden.

Then she caught sight of a figure in the distance and squinted through the windscreen.

It was Gordon.

For a moment it seemed as if she'd gone back in time, for he was wearing the same blue, oil-stained overalls he'd worn when he was her father's apprentice.

Morag looked again, in case she was seeing things.

It was definitely Gordon.

She got out of the car and walked across the grass towards him, but he didn't turn. When she was just a few feet away, she called his name.

He swung round suddenly.

'Morag — is it you?' he asked in disbelief.

'Of course it's me! I got back last night.'

'I can't believe you're back, after all this time! Oh, Morag!'

In an instant he'd taken her in his arms and was kissing her fiercely. Then, just as quickly, he let her go.

'I'm sorry — I had no right.' He raised his hands helplessly and let them fall.

'Why did you stop? I was just beginning to enjoy myself,' she said lightly.

The ghost of a smile flitted over his face at her quick answer.

'Oh, Morag, what a mess I've made of everything!' He sighed. 'Everything I had was tied up in those cars. And your Aunt Olivia has lost the money she invested in me, too.'

'But she was insured. Weren't you?'

'For some of it — but the bulk is owed to the bank. It will take me years to get out of debt.'

Morag stared at him.

Surely Gordon wasn't still putting his business first, after what had just happened between them.

'What are you saying, Gordon? Do you mean that we have to end our

293

relationship because of the fire? Will you be too busy rebuilding your business to have anything to do with me?'

'No! It's not like that. I had to be successful so that I could . . . could . . . '

Morag waited for him to finish, but he turned away.

'Could what?' she prompted.

He still didn't answer.

'Well, let me know when you next have time to see me!' she snapped.

'Morag, please! You mean everything to me! I love you — I've always loved you!' Gordon blurted out.

He put his hands on her shoulders and pulled her close. 'Morag, I want you to marry me . . . ' he murmured.

'Are you sure, Gordon?' she asked sharply.

He nodded.

'Then my answer is yes!' Morag cut in before he could add any qualifications.

He stood open-mouthed, speechless at the speed of her acceptance.

'What is it? Have you changed your mind?' Morag teased.

'But why? I mean, what do I have to offer . . . ?'

'I love you,' Morag said simply. 'The rest of it doesn't matter at all. We'll work through the problems — build the business up again — together.'

'Do you really mean that?' Gordon asked.

'Gordon McEwan, what do I have to do to convince you? You said you wanted to marry me, and I agreed!'

'Morag, you know I love you!' Gordon told her.

He still couldn't quite believe that the one thing he wanted most in life was within his reach.

'Do I? When did you ever tell me before?' she demanded.

'Oh, Morag . . . ' he cried, taking her in his arms again and kissing her.

When they finally drew apart, he took her hand and looked earnestly into her eyes.

'Morag, it won't be easy. I owe the

bank so much. Are you sure?'

'Gordon McEwan, if you say that once again, I'll scream — and I'll tell everyone that you're trying to wriggle out of marrying me!'

Gordon grinned at her.

'We can't have that, can we?' he teased.

Then he took her hand and, holding it, they both turned towards the view which had been a part of their lives for as long as they could remember.

They looked out at the hazy line of hills in the distance, the sloping fields, the row of trees up on the ridge, with rays of sunlight piercing the mist — and at Kilbarton, down in the hollow.

For a moment they gazed silently. Then Gordon gave a little laugh.

'I've been coming up here recently, to stare at this view. You used to love it so much that it made you seem near to me again, when I thought I'd lost you.'

'Lost me? What do you mean?'

'I thought you'd fallen for that Alan Glencairn in Majorca. You were always laughing with him when I phoned.'

'You idiot! Alan was good fun, but there was nothing between us. In fact, I think he's got a soft spot for Cathy. She was really down after Jamie refused to talk to her, but Alan's managed to cheer her up.'

'Is she coming home for Lorna's wedding?'

'I don't know — but I did hint to Alan that he might like to be her partner,' Morag told him.

'She must come for ours — once you name the day,' Gordon said.

* * *

Helen Kinloch paused on her way downstairs to glance at her reflection in the mirror on the landing.

She looked as happy as she felt, she thought to herself. It was a good feeling to like what she saw.

She stopped at the bottom of the stairs, aware of voices coming from the open door of Olivia's room.

'I'm sorry, Tom, but I don't want to hear any more — not until you discuss this with your parents. I don't think they'll like the idea of you competing in car rallies — especially not with your medical history.'

Helen's heart sank. Rallying sounded so dangerous — she hoped it was just a passing craze for Tom.

'But crash helmets are compulsory,' Tom pointed out. 'I'll be fine. Dougie Levington says . . .'

'Dougie Levington! I used to know him — he was competing in rallies when your dad followed them. That was over twenty-five years ago.' Olivia sounded surprised.

'Well, he's still rallying — and he's offered me the chance to train as his navigator,' Tom told her.

'Tom, I won't discuss it until you've spoken to your parents!' Olivia insisted. 'You'll have to get their blessing first.'

Helen had heard enough.

She quietly let herself out of the house, her heart heavy at the thought of

Tom competing in a car rally.

She worried about him so much.

Helen was glad to find Simon alone in his office at Herald Motors. She blurted out what she'd overheard, relieved to be able to share her concerns. But Simon wasn't as sympathetic as she'd hoped.

'It's up to Tom,' he pointed out. 'We can't just wrap him up in cotton-wool for ever, love. He risks being hurt whenever he steps out of the house, but he has to live as normal a life as possible.'

It wasn't what Helen wanted to hear, but she had to agree with Simon's logic. It would be good for Tom to have another interest now that he could no longer play football.

Their conversation was interrupted by Tom, himself, who burst noisily into the office.

'I read in the papers last week that Dougie Levington needed a navigator, so I contacted him,' he said excitedly.

'I know I can't play football in case I

get another knock on the head, but I'll always be wearing a crash helmet when I go rallying.'

'After what happened before, we'd prefer you not to do this,' Simon said, glancing at Helen. 'But I think we both feel it has to be your decision. If you do take up rallying, you'll have to learn to do it properly. And you'll have to finance it on your own.'

'Thanks, Dad — and Mum! I'll do all the homework that's required.' Tom's eyes sparkled with excitement.

* * *

That evening after supper, Helen and Simon settled down in the lounge. It had been a busy day, and they were glad of the opportunity to relax.

'Gordon phoned to say he'll be dropping in tonight,' Helen mentioned. 'Hopefully Morag will be back from Lorna's by then.'

They both looked up at the sound of footsteps on the stairs.

In a moment, Gordon and Morag came in.

'Mum, Dad,' Morag began, looking suddenly shy. 'We've got something to tell you . . .'

Helen and Simon stared at them.

'We're getting married!' Morag blurted out happily.

She didn't need to say another word. The room was filled with handshakes and kisses and laughter as Morag proudly showed off the lovely ring which had belonged to one of Gordon's aunts.

Then Tom hurried downstairs, intrigued by the noise.

'It's about time!' he said as he congratulated Morag and Gordon. 'We'd almost given up on you!'

'Let's all go down and tell Olivia and Jemima the good news,' Helen suggested. She was surprised by how easily the suggestion came to her. Perhaps, at last, she was beginning to forgive her sister-in-law for the past.

They trooped downstairs and found Olivia sitting in her room, reading.

'Oh, what wonderful news!' she exclaimed, once Morag and Gordon had told her of their engagement. 'Jemima, come through here — we've some celebrating to do!

'This calls for champagne!' she announced, turning to Morag. 'I'm so happy for you.'

'It's a pity Cathy's missing all the excitement,' Helen said, after everyone had toasted the happy couple.

'Then why not phone her?' Olivia suggested.

'That's a good idea. Morag, you do it,' Helen suggested. 'She'd love to hear the news from you.'

Morag nodded, pleased to see her mother and Aunt Olivia getting on so well together.

Cathy was ecstatic.

'Oh, Morag, I couldn't be more pleased. You and Gordon were made for each other. Have you set a date yet?'

'Hold on! When I woke up this

morning I never dreamed I'd be celebrating my engagement by evening.'

Morag laughed.

'Once Lorna's wedding is over we'll set the date. I promise we'll let you know when we do!'

'I don't think I'll come home from Majorca for Lorna's wedding,' Cathy said. 'Jamie's still not speaking to me, and I don't want to go on my own.'

'But Lorna will be hurt if you're not there.'

'I know — and I'm sorry. There's Graham, you see,' Cathy pointed out. 'I don't want to risk bumping into him.'

'I don't think that's very likely,' Morag reassured her. 'Lorna told me today that he's gone back to his wife.'

Cathy gulped. She hoped with all her heart that it was true. Perhaps, at last, his obsession with her was over.

'Then I'll definitely think about coming home for Lorna's big day,' she said shakily.

'Don't just think about it,' Morag

said firmly. 'Phone Jamie and get things sorted out.'

'You're right.' Cathy sighed. 'I'll do it.'

An hour later, she had worked up the courage to phone Jamie. She went out into the dusk to use the call-box up on the hill.

She dialled the number and listened to the coins drop as one of Jamie's flatmates answered and went to fetch him.

At last he came to the phone.

Cathy quickly explained her reason for phoning and waited tensely for his reaction.

'Then come to the wedding with someone else,' he said coldly. 'I'm sure you'll have no problem finding another partner.'

Cathy was speechless. It was so unlike Jamie.

'I see — I'm sorry to have troubled you,' she said quietly, replacing the receiver.

She leaned her forehead against the glass at the side of the kiosk and wept.

But she didn't know that Jamie in

Glasgow was shouting, 'Cathy, Cathy!' into the receiver, willing her still to be there. He'd expected her to answer him back — give as good as she got. The old Cathy would have done that without hesitation.

Cathy stood staring down over the rooftops to the harbour, where the lights twinkled and bobbed on the yachts and fishing boats.

She'd brought it all on herself. She'd used people, and lied to them — and then she'd run away in panic to Majorca.

She was walking miserably back down the steep hill to Tibbie's apartment when a figure suddenly came out of the shadows.

'Why are you avoiding me?' Phillipe blocked her path.

She looked at him wearily.

'Phillipe, I can't drop everything when you decide to organise an outing. I'm employed by Mrs Glencairn, remember.'

'You have time off — you could come

then,' he said sulkily.

Cathy felt a pang of apprehension, for the road was deserted. But she was annoyed, too, at Phillipe's refusal to take no for an answer.

'I've told you I don't want to go out with you,' she said firmly.

'That is not an answer.' He refused to move aside to let her pass.

Cathy panicked. She swerved past him and ran, as fast as she could.

As she approached the entrance to the apartments she stumbled into Alan Glencairn.

Alan steadied her and looked up to see Phillipe running after her. He understood what had happened at once. 'You've been told, Phillipe — she wants nothing to do with you,' he said coldly. 'Give it up — now.'

Phillipe glanced from one to the other, then turned away without a word and left them.

'Thanks, Alan,' Cathy sighed in relief. 'He stopped me on my way down the hill.'

She explained about the phone call she had made to Jamie.

Alan listened, then smiled.

'I'm not doing anything then,' he said. 'Would I be an acceptable partner?'

It wasn't such a bad idea. Cathy felt safe with Alan Glencairn, and she enjoyed his company.

Yes, she decided — she'd go to Lorna's wedding, with Alan by her side.

* * *

Two weeks later, on a golden September day, Lorna Stewart, the doctor's daughter, married Max in Kilbarton.

Max and Gordon, the best man, arrived at the church half an hour before the bride. Peggy, who'd worked for the Kinlochs in Kilbarton, was already waiting outside the church.

Her face lit up as the Kinlochs' car drew up.

'That'll be Alan Glencairn,' she whispered to Gordon, pointing to the tall, fair-haired man who helped Cathy out of the car. 'Do you think they'll be the next to get engaged?'

'I haven't a clue!' Gordon laughed at her curiosity.

'Oh, I always liked polka dots!' Peggy was diverted by Helen's outfit. Then she gasped again when she saw Morag.

'You look like a model!' Peggy exclaimed.

As Peggy bustled up the steps into the church, Helen Kinloch noticed Jamie standing to one side, watching Cathy intently. He seemed to flinch visibly when Alan took Cathy's hand, and Helen's heart went out to him.

Being in the church during the service was like a wonderful homecoming for Helen. For over twenty years, the family had worshipped here, and it seemed so right to see Morag and Gordon supporting a radiant Lorna on her wedding day.

Helen still rejoiced over their engagement.

During the signing of the register, she

looked over and saw young Louise Stephens waving enthusiastically to Tom.

'Maybe we'll have another wedding in a few years,' Simon whispered.

'I wonder who Cathy will end up with — Jamie or Alan?' Helen mused.

'Who knows? I don't care, as long as she's happy.' Simon Kinloch smiled down at his wife.

'Maybe she'll be as lucky as I was, and know immediately!' Helen whispered, a nostalgic smile touching her lips.

'And if she's as loyal as her mother,' murmured her husband tenderly, 'he'll be the luckiest man alive — like me!'

Simon clasped Helen's hand in his and, together, they followed the bridal party out into the sunshine, glad that the future offered so much hope and happiness — and love.

We do hope that you have enjoyed reading this large print book.

Did you know that all of our titles are available for purchase?

We publish a wide range of high quality large print books including:
Romances, Mysteries, Classics
General Fiction
Non Fiction and Westerns

Special interest titles available in large print are:
The Little Oxford Dictionary
Music Book, Song Book
Hymn Book, Service Book

Also available from us courtesy of Oxford University Press:
Young Readers' Dictionary
(large print edition)
Young Readers' Thesaurus
(large print edition)

For further information or a free brochure, please contact us at:
Ulverscroft Large Print Books Ltd.,
The Green, Bradgate Road, Anstey,
Leicester, LE7 7FU, England.
Tel: (00 44) **0116 236 4325**
Fax: (00 44) **0116 234 0205**

THE KINDLY LIGHT

Valerie Holmes

Annie Darton's life was happiness itself, living with her father, the lighthouse keeper of Gannet Rock, until an accident changed their lives forever. Forced to move, Annie's path crosses with the attractive stranger, Zachariah Rudd. Shrouded in mystery, undoubtedly hiding something, he becomes steadily more involved in Annie's life, especially when the new lighthouse keeper is murdered. Annie finds herself drawn into the mysteries around her. Only by resolving the past can she look to the future, whatever the cost!

LOVE AND WAR

Joyce Johnson

Alison Dowland is about to marry her childhood sweetheart, Joe, when his regiment is recalled to battle, and American soldiers descend on the tiny Cornish harbour of Porthallack to prepare for the D-day landings. Excitement is high as the villagers prepare to welcome their allies, but to her dismay, Alison falls in love with American Chuck Bartlett. Amidst an agonising personal decision, she is also caught up in espionage, endangering herself and her sister.

OPPOSITES ATTRACT

Chrissie Loveday

Jeb Marlow was not happy to trust his life to the young pilot who was to fly him through a New Zealand mountain range in poor weather. What was more, the pilot was a girl. Though they were attracted, Jacquetta soon realised they lived in different worlds; he had a champagne lifestyle, dashing around the world, and she helped run an isolated fruit farm in New Zealand. Could they ever have any sort of relationship or would their differences always come between them?